C000120131

A SUBTERRANEAN LANDSLIDE
OF HORROR!

The first landfall crashed around them as they crossed the swollen river. As the party made its way deeper into the echoing caverns, Cynthia wondered why they hadn't turned back . . . That foolish young girl had caused the slide with her hysterical shouting. But Albrecht knew the dangers. He had been in and out of this chilling underworld since his boyhood.

Before they started, he had hesitated—then had urged them on with an almost eerie enthusiasm. Never before had he shown such interest in an expedition. But since the incident in the woods—

Where was Albrecht leading them? Was he leading them? What was it that was pulling them down, ever deeper into this world without light?

"No hope of day we find,
Where, unredeemed by light,
We wander, lone and blind,
Within the caves of night."

JOHN CHRISTOPHER

THE CAVES OF NIGHT

AN AVON BOOK

1.

OLD JOACHIM appeared while Henry was signing the register. He took Cynthia's hand and kissed it.

"Gracious lady! And Mr. Herrin—it is a great pleasure to see you both again. Your journey was O.K.?"

"Very O.K.," Cynthia said. She looked about her. The wall plates gleamed as brightly as ever against the dark oak panels. The trophies of the hunt, dominated by the huge boar's head, stared down with the same cozy indifference. "It's lovely to be back, Joachim."

Joachim bellowed something in the dialect, and a lad of fifteen or sixteen appeared from the direction of the kitchen. He was new since their last visit, but he responded as smartly as Joachim's servants always did. Joachim, at least as far as the guests were able to judge, treated them with friendly lenience, but it had occurred to Cynthia before that there might be more to the relationship than lay on the surface.

Henry had finished writing their address and now screwed on the top of his pen and put it away, with his usual unhurried care.

Joachim stationed himself between them. "First, we must drink together—to your health and to our old acquaintance." He urged them in the direction of his private parlor. "This morning I brought up from the cellar the bottle that I bring up only once in the year; and I was thinking that next year maybe it would need to be a new bottle."

Henry said gravely, "Of the same noble stock, one trusts?"

Joachim wagged his head. "Of the things that my father left to me as inheritance, the cellar was put first—even before the inn itself. When the Russians were approaching, I brought the cheap wines and spirits into the first room and covered the door to the second room with rubbish. They did not find it. I despise the Russians."

"For not finding your good wines?"

5

"For thinking that rubbish like that was not a strange thing in an Austrian cellar. It shows in what manner they live in Russia."

Henry said, "And when the English troops came, you took the same precaution?"

Joachim had ushered them into the big, clumsy, comfortable chairs on either side of the window. He went to the cupboard in the wall. He turned around, holding the slender, yellow bottle with the skeletal sprig of herb in it.

"I have been in the infantry myself, you understand. The Queen of Arms gets her living from the land she rules; it is to be expected." He presented a glass to Cynthia before filling the remaining two.

Henry said, "And with the same success?"

"What is that, Mr. Herrin?"

"The rubbish in front of the door deceived the English as well as it had deceived the Russians?"

"Of course!" As the English couple smiled at each other he perceived the implication of his remark. He went on hastily, "But that is not because the English are dirty! It is because they are gentle people, even those in the infantry. If there is wine under their noses, of course they will take it. The Russians ripped open everything in the house, looking for things to take. The English soldiers were not like that."

Henry took the glass that was offered to him. "Whatever the reasons, I join with you in rejoicing at the preservation of your inheritance."

Joachim raised his own glass. "To your country and your health, Mr. and Mrs. Herrin."

"And to yours," Cynthia said. She sipped lightly. "It tastes more wonderful every year."

Henry glanced out the window. The view went down to the swift, shallow waters of the Frohn. Rain was driving across the valley.

"I hear it's been a bad summer," he said.

"Terrible," Joachim agreed. "For many years the worst. The Frohn is nearly a foot above what is to be expected. For a river like the Frohn, that is much."

"But there's still a way clear into the caves?"

"Ah, yes. But they are closed."

Cynthia said, "Oh, no!"

"Closed?" Henry asked. "But why?"

Joachim was chuckling. "You must not worry, Mr. Herrin. For you, I am sure, there will be no difficulty. It is just that you must ask the permission of the Graf."

6

"Graf?"

"At the beginning of the year he was sent back at last from Russia. Everything is being put in order again. Did you not see men working at the *Schloss* as you came by?"

Henry nodded. "I thought it was some Government scheme. And you say he's closed the caves?"

"He did not wish to do so. But there was a fall of rock last winter, and there is thought to be some danger still. It is for that reason he has closed them."

Cynthia asked, "You think he will give permission?"

"I am sure of it. I have spoken to him of the Englishman who comes every year to the Frohnberg caves, and he has said that he would like to meet you. It is for the foolish who are not experienced that the caves are forbidden."

"Then I'd like to make the Graf's acquaintance," Henry said. "The sooner the better."

"That will be seen to," Joachim told them. "Will you have another glass, Mrs. Herrin?"

"Not for me, thank you. I really must see about the unpacking."

Joachim topped up Henry's glass and his own. "If you would grant us just half an hour more, Mrs. Herrin. It is necessary to have your room made ready and the baggage of the other people taken out."

"They're leaving today?"

"No, no." He smiled slyly. "They also are English, and they are on their honeymoon. The husband was stationed here as a young soldier several years ago, and now he has brought his wife. They will stay yet another week, but at the beginning I told them that their room was reserved for you and Mr. Herrin and that when you came they must go into another. They understand all that."

The room had been one of the things to which Cynthia had most looked forward. She could visualize now the way the sunlight shafted in along the valley in the morning to wake them from sleep, and the outlook from the windows: of the green valley of the Frohn, the pine-clad hills on either side, the distant mountains. And the Frohn itself, teeming beneath the slanted roofs of Frohnberg.

She looked quickly at Henry. He shrugged understandingly. She said to Joachim, "No, you mustn't move them. We shall be quite all right in the room you would have put them into."

"Ah, no! That is your room by right."

7

Cynthia said firmly, "I insist. A honeymoon only happens once."

"If at all," Henry said. Joachim looked at him in inquiry. "We were married in wartime," Henry went on. "Forty-eight hours in a hotel in blacked-out London, and we were lucky to get that. Yes, of course they must have the room."

"That is very kind of you," Joachim said. "They will be glad, the young people. And it is only for a week. Then you are in your room again, as before."

The room to which they were shown was quite pleasant. It was smaller than the other, and there was less light in it. The main window looked to the western reaches of the Frohn. There were twin beds in place of the great four-poster.

Joachim, following them in, pointed to these. "They can be changed, if you desire."

Cynthia shook her head. "No. That's perfectly all right. Everything is lovely."

"You are quite sure?" Joachim insisted. "There is nothing that needs to be done?"

Henry, when they were alone, stood by the window. "He's quite right," he commented. "The Frohn's higher than I ever remember. The stakes of the old bridge are under water."

Cynthia glanced up. "Anyway, it's stopped raining."

"An intermission rather than an end. Those clouds look good for several days yet."

Cynthia sighed. "At least, this is Frohnberg, and Joachim's, and there are the caves. Aren't you going along to get washed?"

"Yes, I suppose I should." He rubbed his chin against the back of his hand. "Shave, too, I fancy. You don't want any help with the unpacking?"

Cynthia looked at him in mild exasperation. "You ask me that every year."

"Do I?" He grinned. "I'll head for the bathroom. Throw me my things, will you?"

Cynthia heard her husband whistling his way along the landing. She began transferring clothes from the cases to the large chest of drawers that took up most of the corner between the windows. The drawers were lined with fresh paper and smelled of roses. She bent forward and breathed the scent in deeply.

8

There was a little knock on the door. Expecting one of the maids, she called out, *"Komm herein!"*

She did not turn around immediately when the door opened. A girl's voice behind her said,

"That did mean 'Come in,' didn't it? I'm afraid I still know hardly anything of the language."

Cynthia turned. The girl who stood in the doorway was in her early twenties. Her face was not particularly pretty, but its freshness was striking. She had untidy chestnut hair and a pink and white complexion. Her figure, in a flowery dirndl dress, was slender but mature.

She said, "Mrs. Herrin? I hope you don't mind my barging in like this."

Cynthia said, "Of course not. You and your husband are the other guests, aren't you? Joachim told us about you, but he didn't mention your name."

"I'm Heather Be——" She stumbled on the word, and her color deepened. "Heather Allen. Joachim told me you had insisted on our staying in the room you usually have. It's awfully decent of you. I don't really think we ought to let you. But it's such a dream of a room that I'm going to. I did want to thank you right away."

Cynthia offered her hand. "I'm Cynthia Herrin. Joachim told us you were on your honeymoon. We're old hands here. We know all the views by heart."

"'But don't they grow on you? They must! Peter and I want to come back here again—every year. Even with all this rain, it's been wonderful, and they say generally it's beautifully sunny."

Cynthia nodded. "We've found it so."

"May I sit on the bed?" Heather asked.

"Of course, do."

She lay back on the nearer of the two beds, hands clasped at the nape of her neck. It was an attitude that made her look very young.

"How many years have you been coming to Frohnberg?" she asked.

Cynthia went on with her unpacking. "This is our fifth."

"Is that as long as you've been married?"

Cynthia smiled ruefully. "I'm afraid not. Nowhere near. We've been married sixteen years."

Heather twisted round on the bed. She said anxiously, "Are you happy?"

Cynthia looked at her, two of Henry's shirts on her arm. "Yes. Very. Do I look dissatisfied?"

9

"Lord!" Heather said. "I shouldn't have said that, should I? Of course not. It was just the way you spoke."

There was a stain, Cynthia noted, on the front of one of the shirts. She put it to one side. Frau Klieb, who did the village washing, would see to it.

"Old married couples generally joke about the length of time they've been married, in a specially cynical tone of voice."

"Do they? Do you think I will?"

"Probably. Providing you have a sense of humor."

"Does one need one?"

"It can be useful."

"In making a happy marriage? Mummy used to say something like that. It seems awfully grim, somehow."

"A sense of humor?"

"Having to use it, as though it were some kind of implement, I meant."

Cynthia straightened up and turned around to look at her fully.

"Getting used to things isn't all that unpleasant, you know. It can be quite fun."

Heather said hastily, "Yes! I mean, I'm sure it is. I sent Peter off fishing this afternoon."

"I should think that was very wise," Cynthia said gravely. "He's very fond of fishing?"

"He used to do a lot when he was stationed here in the Army. He talked about it often. So I made sure his rods were packed, and today I insisted that he go and fish." She pivoted on an elbow to gaze out the window. "I hope he hasn't got wet."

Cynthia was amused. "He went willingly?"

"He wouldn't go at first, and then he wanted me to come along as well. But I knew it would spoil things for him if I did. So I told him I had a lot of letters to write." She grinned. "Of course I wouldn't dream of letting anyone think I had time to write letters on our honeymoon; but he never thought of that."

"A man wouldn't," Cynthia said. "You deserve congratulations. I don't think I would have been as sensible when I was your age. There can't be any doubt that you will have a very happy marriage."

Heather said gloomily, "I've been miserable all afternoon."

"But think how nice it will be when he comes back. All this, and a triumphant sense of virtue, too."

"It's starting this business of *contriving* that's so depress-

10

ing. To think that once one's started one has to go on, more and more, for ever and ever. I'll probably be very good at it; I handled him very well today. But that's just the horrible part—handling—finishing up as the kind of woman who manages her husband properly. Only imagine!"

Cynthia said, "I suppose I don't have to."

Heather began, "I didn't mean . . ."

She broke off as the door swung open and Henry came in.

Cynthia said, "This is my husband, Henry. Henry, this is Heather Allen, who's also staying here."

Henry put down the things he was carrying and obediently advanced to shake hands—not only a husband, Cynthia reflected, but unmistakably a managed one. He wore the expression he normally offered to strangers, of insincere politeness. She watched Heather mentally summing him up, with some annoyance.

Heather said, "I must be getting back. There's all sorts of things I've got to do. I only popped in to say thank you for the room. We're awfully grateful."

When she had gone Henry observed, "Honeymoon couples seem to get younger every year."

Cynthia had returned to her unpacking. She said, "She's very nice. She's been explaining to me, in a roundabout way, what an awful prospect it is to have to turn from being a bride into a mere wife."

Henry had gone to stand by the window. He said, "Oh God! One of the frank and friendly brigade."

"But nice. I felt sorry for her."

"For having to turn into a wife?"

"Not exactly. Just for being young, I suppose. One of your shirts has got a stain on it, by the way. I've put it out to be sent to Frau Klieb. You might as well change and toss your dirty things into the basket."

In a leisurely fashion, Henry complied with the suggestion. He said after a pause, "She sounds a bit miserable for a honeymooner. Her new-found husband hasn't abandoned her, has he?"

With the suitcases empty, Cynthia herself had begun to change from her traveling clothes. She unzipped her skirt and stepped out of it.

"As a matter of fact, she drove him off on a fishing expedition. She's practicing wifeliness, and it's been getting her down."

"Frank and friendly *and* talkative," Henry observed. "I

11

think it's a mistake to pity the young for their callowness. It's all part of their colossal self-conceit. Her self-pitying chatter to you doesn't really mean anything. She's as pleased as punch with herself at bottom."

Cynthia pulled on her housecoat. "That's not true—not altogether true, anyway. I'm going to the bathroom. Water hot?"

"What an unnecessary question," Henry said, "in Frohnberg."

When she returned he was still half dressed and leaning forward against the sill of the window. He said, "The sky's a good deal lighter. I don't believe it's going to rain again just yet."

"We could go for a walk by the river before dinner."

"Good idea."

She rested a foot on the bed while she put on a stocking. "Providing you get dressed in time."

Henry turned from the window and began to snap on his suspenders.

"I fancy I saw the missing husband crossing the bridge just now."

"What made you think it was him?"

"His oilskins had a markedly un-Austrian cut."

"What did he look like—young and sporty?"

"Old and decrepit, but that may have been the oilskins."

Cynthia said, "I'm ready. Do get a move on."

They emerged at last from their room onto the landing. Henry, glancing down the stairs, caught his wife's arm. "Voilà! Now you can have a good look at him."

They met on the stairs and stopped for Heather to make introductions. With the oilskins removed, Peter Allen could be seen to be of a little more than average height and stocky in build. He had auburn hair, a gingery mustache, and warily cheerful eyes.

"He caught two trouts," Heather said. She had apparently been waiting at the door for him; Cynthia noticed that she now had a firm grip on one of his arms. "We're going to have them for dinner."

"A very good idea," Henry said.

"Would you like to have one of them? They're not frightfully big, I'm afraid."

Cynthia said, "Thank you. We'll wait for the next catch."

They met Joachim at the foot of the stairs. He said, "Mr. Herrin!"

12

"We thought of taking a walk before dinner, Joachim —along by the river."

"The Graf Frohnberg is here, in my parlor. He hoped that you would be able to speak with him."

"Of course. We'd be delighted."

As they followed the innkeeper, Cynthia murmured, "The village is crowded this season. The nobility and the English. Just like old times."

The Graf got up from one of the chairs as they entered the room; Cynthia was a little disappointed that he did not click his heels. Smiling faintly, he shook hands with them. He had steel-gray hair and a tanned and deeply lined face. She placed him at close to fifty. When he spoke, in English, his voice was only lightly accented.

"I have heard of you," he said, "the English lady and gentleman who return each summer to our caves. You are very welcome to Frohnberg."

Cynthia did not care, she decided, for the hint of feudal patronage in his tone. It was clearly essential, however, to bear with any minor disadvantages if he had the power to ban Henry from his caves.

She said, "We love Frohnberg, quite apart from the caves."

"I hear they've had to be closed," Henry said.

"That is so. There has been a landslip." The faint smile reappeared. "My legal advisers warned me that if any were injured there I might be held responsible."

Henry said, "I was hoping you might be willing to make an exception in my case."

"Yes. I think that is possible. But I should like first to talk with you about it." The Graf lifted his arm and examined a heavy gold chronometer. "Not now, for I am expected back. Perhaps you would do me the honor of having dinner with me this evening."

Surprised by the invitation, they looked at each other. Cynthia said uncertainly, "Joachim—Herr Seifel will have made arrangements already for this evening."

Joachim briskly shook his head. "That is nothing, Mrs. Herrin. Do not think of it."

"I may expect you, then?" the Graf asked. "It is all very informal. There will be yourselves only. I shall be most grateful for your company."

"It's very good of you," Henry said. "What time would you like us to come?"

"Seven-thirty—that will not be inconvenient?"

"Not at all."

13

The Graf shook hands with them both again and left. They heard the rising growl of a high-powered engine shortly afterward.

"Very nice," Cynthia said. "But why, I wonder?"

"I don't know. Surely not simply to talk over whether he's going to let me into the caves or not."

"Perhaps he makes a living selling insurance. If you take out a large policy with his company he'll let you go down."

Henry laughed. "Perhaps. Anyway, we still have time for our walk."

The *Schloss* Frohnberg stood in extensive grounds on the far side of the river from the village. The grounds were enclosed by a high stone wall which opened grudgingly to admit quite a narrow drive. At some time during the military occupation the left-hand post and a section of wall had been destroyed, negligently or deliberately, providing a more convenient ingress for trucks. This, the Herrins noted, had been restored in the last year, and the drive had been leveled and graveled.

The *Schloss* itself was an Italianate mansion, fronted by a broad terrace with steps down to a stretch of lawn, planted with elms, that had clearly once been handsome. Here, however, the ravages of military life had still to be made good. The grass was plentifully scarred with holes and mounds, the usual pock-marks of Army tenure, and in one place there were the faded markings of a football field.

All the same, the view of the house, across the battered lawn, was magnificent.

Cynthia said, "It's not really the sort of place one *walks* up to visit, is it?"

"If one means us, it's not the sort of place we normally visit at all."

"How old would you say he is?"

"The Graf? Forty, or thereabouts."

"I should have said fifty."

"According to Joachim, he's been a Russian prisoner for twelve years. I don't suppose they gave him any special privileges on account of his noble birth."

Cynthia shivered.

"No. What a contrast—to go from this sort of life to that—and then to come back to it again."

Henry gazed speculatively at the building; as the drive

14

curved they could see something of the side as well as the front. There was extensive scaffolding up.

"I don't think it can be insurance," he said. "Unless he owns a company."

They opted, a little uncertainly, for the large front entrance from the terrace, toward which the drive sloped up. A green Mercedes saloon was parked there. Their coats were taken by a manservant, who also showed them into a room leading off the central hall. He explained to them in flat, patient, rather loud German that the Graf would be with them shortly.

The room was of classical dimensions, with a rococo plaster frieze and a ceiling painted with what looked like a florid variation on "The Origin of the Milky Way." The furniture, however, was all contemporary. Almost the whole of one wall was taken up with high double windows, many of them open to the summer twilight. The lighting was also modern; it came from masked strips along three of the walls.

They were craning their necks to make out the details of the ceiling when the Graf came in.

He said, "Good evening. I regret that I was delayed. What can I get you to drink?"

"Sherry, please."

"And you, Mr. Herrin?"

"Scotch, Herr Graf."

The Graf went to a flat glass-fronted cabinet to get the drinks. He said, "My name is Albrecht. I hope you will be kind enough to use that rather than the title."

Henry said, with some awkwardness, "Of course. My wife's name is Cynthia and mine Henry."

"I have been democratized," Albrecht said. "Not by official instruction—they did not think I was worth that— but by experience. I hope it does not embarrass you, being English, to be brought to such terms of intimacy?"

"Not at all."

"It is ludicrous, you see, to be addressed as 'Graf' in the second half of the twentieth century. It has no meaning, in Austria especially. Except, of course, to those Austrians who are foolish enough to cast their eyes backward to 1914."

Cynthia hazarded, "Of course, you're not old enough to remember the old days yourself."

It was difficult to see if he was smiling or not. "Of course."

Henry said, "I take it that our troops left the Schloss in a pretty shocking condition?"

Albrecht shook his head. "Not shocking. I do not think I am capable of being shocked—at least by the acts of Western troops. But it will take some time to restore things, as might be expected. Fortunately my family, before the latest war, was very rich. They were also very ostentatious people, my forebears. They loaded their womenfolk with jewels instead of bonds and banknotes as the sensible ones did. When the Russians were approaching, my mother had the valuables sealed in the wall of one of the stables. It was rather hastily done, but, as frequently happens with such things, it served its purpose as well as the most elaborate preparation. The jewels were recovered after the British occupied these parts. And the sensible ones, with their bonds and banknotes . . ."

Albrecht lifted his empty hands, a gesture the more expressive by reason of the lack of mobility in his normal actions.

"Does your mother live here now?" Cynthia asked.

"She died three years after I was taken to Russia, although I did not learn of her death until my return. There is no one but myself, and I spend much of my time away from Frohnberg. That I am here now is partly because of the harvest, and partly to observe how repairs are progressing."

He glanced at their glasses. "Will you have more to drink before we go in to dinner?" The Herrins shook their heads. "Let us go, in that case."

It was not until after dinner that the question of the caves was raised. They had coffee in the library; Albrecht apologized for the bareness of the shelves.

"The books disappeared in circumstances about which I am badly informed. As between being shipped home by a profiteering senior officer and being burned to keep the ordinary soldiers warm in our Frohnberg winters, I am inclined to hope it was the latter. I do not think that I shall make any attempt to restock the shelves. I fancy that reading as an occupation may be on its way back to the schools and the monasteries."

Cynthia said, "And you don't believe in swimming against the tide?"

"Having encountered the kind of tide that will have no opposition, there is little pleasure in battling against lesser ones. Brandy?" Cynthia showed her refusal. "But you will have one, Henry."

16

Albrecht brought the glass over. "Now, your caves. I should like to know about them. First I will tell you what I know. That the Frohn springs out of the Frohnberg, plainly. That in the summer, when the water level is less high, one can walk into the cave from which it flows. The children have always played there. Also, that one may climb up the slope at the cave's end, and find a grotto, with stalactites and so on. That was where the more daring children played."

"Where was the rock fall?" Henry asked.

"At the entrance. It has been wired off, and there is a gate which is kept locked."

"Was it a heavy fall?"

"No. But my land steward is uneasy about the condition of the rest. He is a man to whom uneasiness is natural; I remember that he once suspected Dollfuss of being Anti-Christ. But one does not like to take chances where children are concerned. Now, tell me how you came to be interested in the caves."

"I've been a pot-holer since I was at Cambridge," Henry said. "I've done quite a bit of it in England and Wales, and a little in France. Then five years ago we came for a holiday to Austria—to Graz, actually. Someone mentioned the Frohnberg caves, knowing I was interested in caves. I was told there wasn't much to them—that the important caves were at Liedl, on the other side of the hills—but we thought it might be worth a run up here. Liedl was more difficult to get to."

Albrecht nodded. "From Graz, yes. You went to Liedl at a later time?"

"Not that year. I went up there on our second visit to your country, but I found the Liedl caves disappointing. They are bigger, of course, and more extensive, but I can't summon up much interest in caves that have electric light installed. And meanwhile I had found that there was more to the Frohnberg caves than the first two chambers."

"Yes, that is what interests me. Please go on."

"You know the ledge that runs around the left-hand side of the grotto?"

"Yes."

"The wall is sheer there. Above head height it's difficult to bring a light to bear on it, because the ledge you are standing on is so narrow. I had my hands over my head, feeling for any sign of carving reliefs on the wall, and I found a hole. All I could tell then was that there was a break in the rock face, two or three feet across. The fol-

17

lowing day I took in a ladder. I found that the hole was a chimney, and not a particularly difficult climb, either."

"And it led you to—?"

"Another chamber, bigger than the first two."

Albrecht replenished his own glass and Henry's. "You made this discovery five years ago?"

"Yes."

"And you have since explored what lies beyond the chimney?"

"Only to a limited extent. There is a route which takes you down to the level of the Frohn again, and you can follow the river in for some distance. There's another grotto about fifty yards along with a very pretty display of gypsum flowers. One could probably penetrate a good deal farther, I imagine."

"But you have not done so?"

"So far I've been too interested in the chamber immediately beyond the chimney. It's of considerable size, as I've said, and there's quite a good showing of paintings on the walls."

"Cave paintings? Here in Frohnberg? My land steward did not tell me anything of this."

"I'm afraid I kept quiet deliberately. I can only get here for a fortnight a year. This is the only speleological discovery I've ever made, and I wanted to keep it to myself as far as possible. I persuaded myself that paintings which have waited tens of thousands of years for discovery could wait a few more years before going on display. Now, of course, that is for you to decide."

"I should like to see them," Albrecht said. "Other than that, I prefer that they should be left in your hands. I have no feeling for art, one way or another."

Cynthia asked, "Isn't that a Van Eyck on the wall over there?"

The smile touched his lips. "If one looks at it from such a distance, yes. If one stands close and examines it by means of a magnifying glass, it will prove to be a clever reproduction. In the *Alte Pinakothek* at Munich one may see the genuine canvas, and if it were for sale one would require—let me see—twenty thousand pounds to buy it. The painting which hangs on my wall I bought for less than ten pounds in Vienna."

"But you did choose it."

Albrecht shrugged. "I like it. It is a pleasant scene. Perhaps it is also a work of art. I am curious to see Henry's

18

cave paintings. It does not seem to me that I have any responsibility toward them."

"I should finish what I need to do on them this year," Henry said. "Do you have any objection to my writing them up after that? I don't think they are particularly important as cave paintings—nothing like Altamira or the other major sites—but they may bring a few people along."

"It will give Adolf, my steward, something on which to exercise his worries. As I have told you, I am not here much."

Cynthia stretched back into the sensuously enclosing chair in which she sat. It was of modern design, shaped something like a large shell, but upholstered in crimson plush.

"Do you have business in Vienna, Albrecht?"

He stared at her. "My business is pleasure. Vienna is a good place to pursue it. But I go elsewhere. I have recently returned from Italy."

She asked him, "How does one measure success in that kind of business?"

"As in others—by the increase in expertness and the decrease in satisfaction. And, of course, by the growing dread of retirement."

Henry smiled. "Yes. But since you speak of retirement, I think we must prepare for ours. It's close on eleven and —if I have your permission—I should like to tackle the caves early in the morning."

"No more brandy before you go? In that case, I will give you the key to the gate Adolf put up." Albrecht went across to one of the empty shelves and opened a small box. "Yes, here it is. Adolf also has one, and I have a third. You will not object if I visit you during your work?"

"We'd be delighted."

"Cynthia is also a student of cave paintings, then?"

"When she feels like it. She nobly puts up with my pot-holing, at any rate."

"I like walking in the hills," Cynthia said, "or just lazing in the sunshine. There has been sunshine other summers. I'm very fond of Frohenberg."

"I hope you will make free of this house and the grounds while you are here," Albrecht said, "both of you. And now, since it is late, I will drive you back to the inn."

Henry protested. "It's no distance. Barely half a mile."

"I insist."

19

2.

THE ALLENS were just coming down to break-fast as they prepared to leave the following morning. Heather stared curiously at them. They were wearing old clothes, and Cynthia had on trousers and jersey.

"Golly, you two are off early! Oh, I suppose you're going up to the caves? Joachim said something about them. Could we come along later?"

Henry said, "If you want to see them, we'll ask the Graf for you."

"Does one have to?"

"He's had them closed because of a landslip. Probably he will have no objection, but we must ask him first."

"Are they dreadfully exciting, like Cheddar and Wookey Hole?"

Henry shook his head. "No. Rather dull." He glanced at Heather's silk blouse, gabardine skirt and nylon stockings. "And to get there you have to crawl through a funnel about three feet across, quite apart from walking through the Frohn."

"It sounds ghastly," Heather said. "We'll have to think it over." She sniffed in the direction of the kitchen. "Just now, all I can really think about is food. Since we've been here I've simply done nothing but eat."

As they walked out into the broad street which more or less made up the village, Cynthia said, "Look at that sky."

It was deep blue, unspecked. The ground rose in the direction which they were taking, and where the road bore left under the lee of the Frohnberg the roofs of the houses were sharp against the azure.

"If it lasts," Henry said. "Visibility's a little too good. Still, we should be all right for the morning."

"Probably be clear while we're inside the hill, and clouding up by the time we come out."

"You could stay outside and make the best of it."

"I want to see you settled in first. I may come out again then and do a bit of climbing."

Henry grinned. "You could collect the Allens."

20

"Do you think they will want to go through into the caves?"

"I doubt it. I think I put her off, don't you?"

"You did your best. Don't you like them?"

"I'm like Albrecht with art—no feeling one way or the other. Except that they strike me as a bit absurd."

"Absurd? Why?"

"Being honeymooners, I suppose. Isn't it natural to laugh at them?"

"Yes, I suppose so. But there's something rather nice as well as absurd about it."

They crossed the road. Here, on the left, was the sweep of the hill behind the houses. A cart track between two of them led steeply upward; one could climb over the spur as a short cut, rejoining the road, or the River Frohn, on the other side of the bend.

The grass under their feet was heavy with dew. Spiders' webs glistened on the bushes. As they climbed up the green slope, the roofs of the village dwindled to the size of toys, and the Frohn, tumbling silver through the valley below, came into sight.

Cynthia paused by the big jutting boulder where they generally stopped for a minute or two. She pointed to the *Schloss*, regnant among its lawns and trees on the far side of the river. "He's very lucky, isn't he?"

"Albrecht? He struck me as a bit of a puzzle."

"In what way?"

"Inviting us to dinner practically as soon as we met—telling us so much about his personal affairs—and this business of posing as the rich idler."

"Do you think it's a pose?"

"He was too cynical about it. The genuine hedonist doesn't operate on the intellectual level."

Cynthia smiled. "How many genuinely hedonistic Austrian counts have you met?"

"How did he strike you?"

"I've told you—lucky. To come back from a Russian prison camp to an estate like this and find that there's enough cash in the till to keep it going in something like the prewar style . . . it's a kind of resurrection, I should think."

"Very satisfactory from my point of view, anyway. A more orthodox landlord might have had more positive views on the caves. Ready to push on?"

The hill began to be wooded at this point. They climbed through the thickening scatter of trees to the crest of the

21

ridge and then made their way down the other side. As the trees thinned out again, they could see the end of the valley, where the Graz road threaded its way through a narrowing defile. Immediately below them the Frohn foamed under the first of its many bridges; nearer still, hidden by the hill's overhang, was the cave from which it issued.

The last hundred yards was something of a scramble. They came up against a stout picket fence, anchored on one side to the hill and on the other projecting into the river. The gate in the middle of it was heavily padlocked.

As Henry unlocked the gate with the key Albrecht had given him, a jackdaw swooped low along the surface of the river and darted under the arch of rock. Henry pointed to it.

"Our old friend hasn't abandoned us."

To the right, the emerging river foamed, deep and urgent, against the rock. It was on the left that there was a ledge along which entry was possible. The cave, however, was on the other side of the river; as the ledge dwindled and finally disappeared, it became necessary to wade across. The Herrins, before going in, put on the rubber boots they had brought with them.

Henry said, "She's quite a bit higher than usual. You will have to walk carefully if you aren't going to get a bootful of water."

Looking distastefully at the tumbling water, silver in the sunshine but grimly black under the arch of rock, Cynthia said, "I'll be careful. It's damnably unfair my having short legs."

Henry grinned at her. "I don't know. I probably would never have married you otherwise. I can't bear long-legged women."

"I'll try to count that as a blessing. It won't be easy if I get a soaking in there."

The first signs of the landslip were evident less than ten yards inside the arch. The wall had fallen in, and in place of the ledge there was a sloping pile of rubble. Henry examined this with interest.

"I always thought that wall was pretty firm. Probably our best move is to take to the water here. It only means a few more yards of wading."

"You first."

Henry slipped over the edge into the river. It was deeper than it was farther in. The water came to within six inches of the top of his boots. It hissed around them as though it were boiling.

22

Cynthia said decisively, "I'll take the rubble. You can stand by ready to catch me if I slip down."

The loose stones and earth began to slide as Cynthia scrambled across the slope, and those at the bottom racketed into the water. The bulk held, however, and she managed to reach the continuance of the ledge on the other side. Henry waded forward against the current. The rock roof, which had been several feet above their heads at the entrance, began to slope downward. As far as the Frohn itself was concerned, the slope was continuous to the point, perhaps thirty yards inside, where roof and water joined.

The cave proper lay on the right; a hole two or three feet above the surface of the water rapidly widened. Here Cynthia had to take to the water; she trod warily, with Henry supporting her. In midstream there was barely an inch of clearance between her boot tops and the water.

Henry heaved himself through the hole, having first taken off his pack and tossed that through, and then reached back to pull his wife after him. He flashed the broad beam of his torch into the cave.

"There doesn't seem to be anything wrong here. It may have been only a small local slip."

"Take things carefully, all the same."

"Don't I always?"

Their voices, as usual, echoed strangely from the walls of rock all around them. They advanced up the slanting floor of the cave. At the top they wriggled through the gap of about two feet between the opposing jaws of rock and came out into the grotto.

The grotto was roughly circular and about thirty feet across. The roof soared to a point beyond the effective range of torchlight. The steady drip of water was louder here than the distant rushing of the Frohn. Parallel with one wall, a palisade of stalactites stabbed downward to within a foot of the rocky floor.

The torch beam fastened on the small wooden ladder which Henry had left from earlier years. He had not thought it worth the trouble to take it back to the village; on the other hand, he had left it by the stalactite palisade rather than in position at the chimney, to make it less likely that anyone venturing in should repeat his own discovery.

He carried the ladder over to the far wall and wedged it in place. Then he climbed up and, pushing his pack ahead

23

of him, heaved himself into the chimney. Cynthia followed.

She said, "This is the part I really don't like. I think I get the shivers more every time I go through it."

The chimney was about ten feet long. In the center it narrowed, but then it broadened again and continued to broaden until it came out as a fair-sized hole in the middle of the floor of the next cave. She hauled herself up behind Henry and waited while he found the acetylene lamp in his pack and lit it.

The light flared up to illuminate a cavern half as big again as the one from which they had come. Henry swung the lamp around in an examining arc. He pointed down the slope that led eventually to the underground reach of the Frohn.

"There have been other falls. Look down there." There was a new rubble pile, of considerable extent and above an average man's height. "At least the walls are clear. We can spare a section of roof. It's too high to have any paintings on it."

Cynthia said, "You might have been standing underneath when it came down. You wouldn't have had much chance in that case."

Henry was removing the remainder of his gear from the pack. "The odds are against it. It must have been the heavy frosts they had around here last winter. It probably cracked the rock."

"I thought this part was well inside the hill."

"Yes, it is. There may have been a crack higher up which started a small fault. That would account for there being falls in several places—very likely along the line of the fault."

"Then it may be still dangerous."

"It should have had time enough to settle down. As long as we don't go about shouting our heads off or indulge in violent gymnastics, I should think it would be all right."

He walked over, holding the light, to examine the nearest wall.

Cynthia followed him. "I'm not happy about it."

"Nothing to worry about. The old bison's still untouched." He peered forward, tracing the smears of red and brown paint that formed the animal. "Isn't he a beauty?"

Cynthia said sharply: "What's that?"

Henry listened. "The Frohn. A bit noisier than usual with being in spate."

24

"No, something else. Listen."

It was a dull scratching sound. Henry cocked his ear to it and then walked back toward the middle of the cave. He bent over and called down the chimney, "Can you manage all right?"

Albrecht's muffled voice came up to them. "Thank you, yes."

Henry held the lamp over the hole. In a moment Albrecht's silver-gray head emerged from the chimney's constriction, and shortly afterward he hauled himself out to stand beside them.

"Not the most comfortable route," he observed. "You have found no other way into this cave?"

"No. I'm pretty sure there isn't one. Caves that have paintings are normally difficult to get at. There are several which are much harder than this to reach."

"I did not know that. So even our prehistoric ancestors preferred to reach their really important goals the hard way? Folly has a long history."

Henry led the way over to the painting of the bison. "This is my favorite. See the foreshortening effect with that slope of the spine away from the neck? They knew more about perspective than modern man did five hundred years ago."

"Yes. The flank is badly worn—by erosion?"

"No, by spear jabs and arrows. That's the magic part of it—to bring them success in hunting. The Australian aborigines still do it."

"And does it work?"

"A good hunter is always likely to succeed, and the more confident he is the more successful he's likely to be."

"That is certain." Albrecht flashed his own torch along the wall. "And this? A man?"

"No. A bear."

"I see it. It is badly worn, though. They were fond of bear meat, our ancestors?"

"It wasn't only that. They had to share the caves with the bears. Even a good hunter would need a very heavy dose of self-confidence to be prepared to tackle a bear in a narrow tunnel underground. I should think they were very fond of bear meat; every mouthful would be a separate triumph."

They made the round of the paintings. Henry said, "As you see, not a particularly striking collection. There are a few more, high up at the far end. I shall have to rig up some sort of platform to examine those."

25

Albrecht pointed down the slope of the cave. "And in that direction one finds the Frohn again? That is the noise, I take it?"

"Yes, that's the Frohn. I haven't been down there today. Do you want to have a look? The going is a bit difficult, and of course I don't know whether there have been any falls down there."

"I will wait until another time. I find that caves do not excite me as much as they did when I was a boy. I will leave you to your studies."

"Perhaps you could take Cynthia with you," Henry said. "She only came along to see that I got settled in. Fording the river is a little tricky for her since it's so high."

Albrecht nodded. "I shall be delighted."

Cynthia said, "Are you sure you'll be all right here? I'm still not happy about the rock falls."

"I shall be working by the walls, and they're all very solid. If there is going to be a fall, it's much more likely to be set off by three of us talking in the middle of the cave." He bent down and gave her a brief parting kiss. "You two go back and enjoy the sunshine."

"I will go first," Albrecht said. "Then I can help you at the bottom of the chimney."

They made their way back through the two outer caves to where the river waters bubbled and eddied.

Cynthia said, "You go first again, if you don't mind. I shall have to ease myself into the water very carefully. I nearly got my legs flooded on the way in."

Albrecht slid backwards into the river. "If you do not mind, I think it will be best if I carry you."

"The roof's very low."

"Not too low, I fancy. If you come down feet first, and put your feet through the crook of my arms, and if we both then keep our heads bent, I do not think there will be any difficulty."

It was hardly possible, Cynthia reflected, to raise her real objection to the plan—that Albrecht, at his age, did not inspire confidence in his abilities as a porter across an underground river. In any case, even if she got a ducking, they were on their way out; it was a sunny day and it would not take her long to get back to the inn. She did as he had told her. His arms tightened over her legs, and he bent his head so that she could rest her own head forward on the back of his neck. Then he stepped out into the stream.

26

She realized at once that he was stronger and fitter than he looked. He waded steadily and surely downstream, bending far forward where the roof dipped, and they were soon at the ledge beyond the landslip. He helped her onto it and then climbed up himself. The white glow of daylight ahead enlarged itself into the harshness of sunlight. They stood and blinked their eyes to reaccustom them.

Albrecht asked her, "You had made plans as to what you would do this morning?"

"I thought I might go for a walk. It's such a lovely day."

The inquiry was innocent enough, but it had made her conscious, for the first time, of the possibility that Albrecht might attempt to make love to her. As a professed hedonist, he might even regard it as expected of him. The possibility would account for his unexpectedly friendly interest in the visiting English couple. She began to devise parrying answers against an offer to show her the countryside.

Instead, he said, "My own interest in nature is quite static. I can sit and watch, but I do not care to walk about and watch. For exercise I prefer games. Do you play games, Cynthia?"

The question was so palpably innocent of any double meaning that she almost smiled. "Tennis, a little."

"I, too, enjoy tennis. They have finished re-laying the courts. You would not care to play there this morning?" She hesitated. "Unless you have set your mind on your walk."

She realized that her speculation of a few moments earlier could be accounted for to a large extent by her surprise at finding Albrecht so much stronger physically than she had expected. That, she thought ruefully, and schoolgirl stories about dissolute Counts and their exercise of *droit du seigneur*.

"I should love to," she told him.

"Excellent!"

"I haven't any proper clothes, though."

Albrecht closed the gate behind them and locked it. "That has no importance. Up here. I have the car on the other side of the road, by the bridge."

"Will you drop me at the inn first? I can make some attempt to dress suitably. At least I can find a blouse and skirt, and some canvas shoes."

As he settled himself into the driving seat, he made her suspicions seem utterly unworthy by saying. "The young

27

couple who are staying at the inn—do you think they might also wish to play?"

"I've no idea. I suppose they might."

"If they have not gone out, you can ask them. I should be honored to have them join us."

On Albrecht's suggestion, Cynthia introduced the Allens to him on first-name terms. They got into the back of the Mercedes, and the car pulled smoothly away, scattering the loose stones outside the door of the inn.

Albrecht said, "Joachim has told me that you have already been a guest at my house, Peter?"

Peter said, "Yes. That's why we came here. I'm afraid you must have found things in a shocking mess."

"No. Less bad than I had expected. I was glad to find four walls and a roof."

"We had a shot at getting the swimming pool and the tennis courts back into shape," Peter said, reminiscing.

"Yes. My steward discovered two Louis Quinze chairs in the pavilion."

"Good God! Were they? I remember those chairs."

Albrecht eased the Mercedes through the entrance to the *Schloss* grounds. "An overrated school of furniture," he commented. "If only our insurance brokers had survived the war, I should have welcomed their destruction."

The tennis courts were some distance from the main buildings, with the swimming pool—an unusually long oblong constructed entirely of wood—almost adjacent. Both were surrounded by tall shrubs; these were in full leaf now, and made a complete screen. There was a strong smell of verbena. The pavilion that Albrecht had spoken of lay between the courts and the pool, giving access to each.

They played two sets of mixed doubles. When Heather suggested a third, Albrecht declined courteously. "I hope you will excuse me. I am past the age at which it is not important to conserve the energies."

Cynthia said, "I'll drop out, too. You two can play singles."

"Single-doubles," Heather said. "Peter can play against us."

"No, I'd really rather rest." She smiled at Albrecht. "I'm past the age, too."

"That is absurd," Albrecht said, "but I shall be glad to have you as a partner in resting. We will order drinks.

Perhaps that will tempt these young people from the court."

He gave his order over the telephone and then came and sat beside Cynthia. Heather's tennis was of a desperate character; she chased from side to side of the court retrieving her husband's well-placed shots. Albrecht watched with grave but apparent enjoyment. When she succeeded in winning a rally, he applauded.

Cynthia framed the comment once in her mind, and withdrew it without utterance. It would represent a voluntary act of engagement on her part, and for a moment she was afraid of the engagement—or rather of its possibilities. It was in deliberate reply to that fear—a refusal to be intimidated by her own unreasonable intuition—that she framed it again, and this time spoke.

"You are a strange person, Albrecht."

His eyes turned to hers, as though in polite inquiry.

"Do you think so? I believe that myself, of course, but it is natural that I should. We are strangers to ourselves first; to others only at second hand. What is it in me that you find strange?"

"I suppose the really odd thing is the way you have behaved toward us."

"Have I offended you?"

"Of course not. Quite the opposite. It's your hospitality that seems surprising."

"It is difficult to believe that the English find hospitality a strange thing."

"Toward people quite unknown, who are not even your countrymen?"

"I am interested in human beings; here at Frohnberg, which it was necessary for me to visit, there are only the servants. You do me service by giving me your company."

"But Frohnberg is your home—you were born and reared here."

"You have forgotten that this took place in the days of what my Russian hosts called reactionary land-owning capitalism. My neighbors were not the peasants but the other fascist landlords. Very few of them have survived the upheaval, and those that have no longer live here in Styria."

"But you must have made new friends since you came back from Russia."

"Must I? Ah, here is Hans, with the drinks!" He spoke rapidly in German, and Hans set down the tray on the table beside their chairs and left. "I shall have lime juice

29

and soda, but there are also orange and lemon drinks, and vodka which can be added if you wish."

"I'll have lime juice and soda, too, please."

Albrecht poured drinks for them both. He gestured with his glass toward the players. "Are they not charming? Surely, of all the delights that the mingling of the sexes can give, there is none to compare with that of the newly wed. All is brilliance about them. They move through a world that transcends the world. Do not agree?"

"It isn't always as happy a time as it looks from outside."

"But of course not! From inside it must have its terrors and torments, and worse than that, perhaps—the monotone of dissatisfaction. A puppy's world is not that absurd and happy world in which we see the puppy stumble along. But there is the illusion that the observer sees, and perhaps they glimpse it, also, reflected in our eyes."

"You have never married?"

"No. I have never married." There was a humorous finality in his tone, as though he were accepting a pronouncement that condemned him to a celibate old age.

Cynthia added, "But you will marry?"

He shook his head. "No."

She was not happy about the turn of intimacy which the conversation had taken, but saw no way of going back.

She asked him, "Your family have lived here for hundreds of years. Don't you wish to have sons and grandsons living here after you?"

He moved to face her. "The illusion of that desire tormented me for longer than a year, during the time I was a prisoner. It was the fifth year, I think. Most of those who had been prisoners with me had been sent back to their countries. It was then that I began to think I would die in Russia—from old age, if in no other way. And the worst agony was thinking that there would be no more von Frohnbergs here in Frohnberg. Is that not strange?"

Cynthia returned his look. "No. I don't think so. Why did you say illusion of desire?"

"What else was it? It passed, and passed so completely that now, when there might be a hope of satisfaction, it does not return."

"It's the second time you've spoken of illusion, within a few minutes. Do you think all desires are illusions then?"

"I only know my own."

She said nothing, choosing silence rather than to risk the hazards of an uncharted philosophical sea. The pause

30

continued for some moments, before Albrecht said, "They are tireless, are they not?"

She laughed. "Even the sight of the drinks hasn't lured them in!"

Albrecht unexpectedly stood up. He extended a hand toward her. "Come. I will show you something of the park."

She had half risen before the thought of refusal crossed her mind. She said, her voice made formal by uncertainty, "Thank you. I'd be glad to."

Albrecht led her through the pavilion and they came out beside the swimming pool. The wood had been painted turquoise blue, and the water took this color from it. It shimmered with odd lights in the direct brilliance of sunshine. There was a three-stage diving board at one end, and a springboard, covered with blue matting, beside it.

"I've never seen a wooden swimming pool before," Cynthia said.

"Styria is a land of timber. We make many things of wood."

He touched her elbow to guide her away from the pool; his hand was rough against her flesh. They walked through the shrubbery and came out into the parkland which made up the greater part of the *Schloss* grounds. High trees were decently spaced among recently scythed grass. The smell of verbena came only in gusts now, and for that reason seemed the more fragrant.

Albrecht was leading her away from the *Schloss* toward a small round brick structure topped by a high pinnacle of blue slates. There was a leaded window in the part of the wall nearest to them.

"It looks older than the *Schloss*," she said. "What is it?"

"It is much older than the *Schloss* which now stands. As to what it is—that you will shortly see. I do not think you have such things in England."

As they drew nearer she saw that much of the building was sunk below ground level. To one side there was a short flight of stone steps, leading down. She followed Albrecht. A heavy wooden door was secured by an iron ring; he turned this and the door swung open. Then he stood by, indicating that she should come forward to look inside.

She looked, and drew back in the same instant. The interior was like that of a very small chapel; and it was full of a jumble of bones. Almost at her feet a skull rested, staring upward out of blind sockets. Other skulls were scattered all over the floor, mixed in with a welter of arm

31

and leg bones, and other bones less easily identified. Some of them were broken; one skull was cracked in half.

Albrecht was looking at her, with a distant polite smile. She shook her head. "I don't understand. What are they doing here?"

"They are here by right," Albrecht said gently. "This is their home, as Frohnberg was when they were alive. They died and were buried, and when the flesh had quite rotted off their bones, their bones were brought here, to rest until the Day of Wrath."

"But surely not like that—just scattered on the floor!"

"Indeed, no. Not in Austria. They were placed in neat piles, the long bones in one place and the skulls in another. One supposes that the soldiers thought there might be gold hidden among them."

"But aren't you going to restore them?"

"Yes. But they can wait until the other work has been done. They are not impatient."

He closed the door to the vault. She stood, waiting for him to lead the way back up the steps. Instead he put his hands on her shoulders. With a shock of unruly pleasure she felt his strength as he pulled her toward him, but she turned her face away. He kissed her cheek. She remained quite still, and he released her.

She asked, "Why did you do that?"

"Because I wanted to do it. You are a lovely woman, of much charm, and it is as reasonable to want to kiss you as it is to admire you."

"I'm also a married woman."

"Of course. If such a kiss is thought innocent, then it makes no difference that you are married. If not innocent, surely it can do less harm than to an inexperienced girl."

Shock began to turn to anger. She said in a hard voice, "Did you expect me to respond?"

"Believe me, gracious lady, I expected nothing. Expectation is another part of illusion, and I have none left. I wanted to kiss you—that is all. Shall we go up, into the sunlight?"

The ludicrousness of the situation suddenly struck her, dispelling shock and anger alike. She forced back an impulse to smile. As she walked beside Albrecht up the steps, she asked, "Do you usually make advances to the other sex in such forbidding surroundings?"

Albrecht smiled slowly. "Was it that—advances to the other sex? That is an English way of putting it? But I do not usually take ladies to see the bones of my ancestors."

32

"Why did you take me?"

He looked at her intently. "I do not know. Perhaps because you are English, and this is a custom that would be strange to you. Or perhaps . . . No, I do not know."

They walked together in silence through the trees and the sun-speckled grass. It surprised Cynthia that she had no sense of strain existing between them. This was not the first time since she had married Henry that it had been necessary to stop a man from making love to her, but always with the others her refusal had created an awkwardness that could only be dispelled by the man's leaving or by the arrival of others. There was no such awkwardness now.

They were approaching the tennis courts. Albrecht pointed to them, indicating their emptiness. "See, the game is over."

HENRY AND PETER were downstairs in the big parlor, drinking beer. The two women had gone up to freshen themselves before dinner, and now sat talking in the Allens' bedroom. The day had ended as clear as it had begun; all the Frohn valley was lit with the afterglow of sunlight.

Heather, sitting on the small stool in front of the dressing table, stretched her arms, elbows jutting upward, and groaned.

"I am an idiot! Peter didn't want to play that last set but I insisted. I shall be stiff as a board for days."

Cynthia was standing by the window, looking out. All the near landscape—the fall of houses to the river, the river itself and the *Schloss* beyond—was dark against the luminous crestline of the hills. Without turning around she said, "Joachim's bound to have some kind of liniment. Would you like me to get some and rub it in for you?"

Heather lifted one wrist to look at her watch. "There isn't really time before dinner. We can ask him afterward." She flexed her body sensuously. "Peter can give me a rub before we go to bed."

"Just like an old married couple," Cynthia observed.

33

Heather giggled. "I doubt if it will be!" Something seemed to strike her, and she looked toward Cynthia. "Do you think it's a bad thing to do?" she appealed.

"It probably depends on the liniment. If you can get Joachim to provide you with one smelling of roses or pine, it should be all right."

"Sometimes," Heather said, "I wish I were a widow."

Cynthia was too surprised to do more than echo her. "A widow?"

"No, I don't mean that! It's just that second honeymoons must be quite as nice as first, and so much less trouble. One knows it all by then."

"You'll have to wait a few years and come back for your second honeymoon, in that case."

"I didn't mean with the same husband."

Cynthia laughed. "Then you will have to ask Peter very nicely, and perhaps . . ."

Heather sighed. "I'm about incoherent, aren't I? It's just the unfairness of things I'm complaining about. You can never have it all, and I want it all. Anyway, fat lot of chance of a second honeymoon there'll be, even with Peter. You can't go around honeymooning with a swarm of kids crawling all over you."

"You're going to have a swarm of kids?"

"I was working out the other day," Heather said, "that I could just possibly have two dozen—that's not allowing for twins and things. But I think I'll stop at six."

"That's a fair allowance," Cynthia said, "for someone who's scared stiff of learning how to manage her husband."

Heather had taken up a brush and had begun to put order into her unruly hair, shaking her head from side to side as she did so. She paused, the brush still holding her locks, turning her head around in Cynthia's direction.

"No, but that's just it. If I've got to stop being—well, I suppose you call it a bride—I must have something else to make up for it. Don't you feel like that?"

"No."

"Didn't you want to have children at all?"

The use of the past tense, although probably more a matter of Heather's customary bad phrasing than thoughtlessness, hurt her.

"I suppose we got into the habit of not having them. Henry's sisters and my brother are very prolific, so we have a good supply of nephews and nieces. We both like

34

the arrangement, and it means we can get about together without any difficulty."

She cut herself off abruptly, and stared down into the darkening valley. The blow must have been more solid than she had thought, to provoke her into such a justification. She wondered if she could possibly, in any way, be envying Heather. The idea, when openly examined, was ridiculous, of course.

"Probably you're right," Heather said amiably. "When I'm being brought to bed for the sixth time, I'm sure I'll think you are."

Cynthia said nothing. Heather went on: "Albrecht is nice. Don't you think so?"

"Provided he doesn't get you on your own."

She was disgusted with herself as soon as the words were out; not only in the discovery of herself saying them, but in the realization that she had so largely been prompted by a whim to impress Heather, to brandish her little sexual triumph before the younger woman.

Heather said excitedly, "No! Is he? What happened? Do tell."

She said reluctantly, "Nothing much."

"When and where? It must have been when he took you off in the park while we were playing tennis. Darling, you must tell! I'll get such a fevered imagination about it if you don't."

"You're on your honeymoon," Cynthia reminded her. "And I thought you wanted to pass straight from bride to mother of six. You haven't got other ambitions as well, have you?"

"Don't be beastly. One can't help being *interested*."

"I've told you—it wasn't much. He tried to kiss me." She smiled slightly. "Just after he had shown me the family skeletons."

"What a lovely bit of gruel Did you slap his face, or bite him, or something?"

Cynthia shook her head. "I didn't do a thing. With anything short of a maniac, doing nothing is the most effective thing you can do."

"Is it? I suppose he thought you were the usual cold-blooded Englishwoman. He let you go?"

"Yes."

"Do you think he'll try again?"

Cynthia looked at her with slight exasperation. "You seem to find it all tremendously interesting."

"Of course I do! Are you going to tell Henry about it?"

35

"Would you tell Peter?"

Heather considered for a moment. "No, I wouldn't. I couldn't trust him not to burst out laughing the next time we saw Albrecht. Of course, Henry isn't like that."

"Not a bit."

"Are you going to tell him?"

"I haven't made up my mind yet."

"What did you do other times?"

"What other times?"

"When you were learning that about doing nothing being the best thing to do."

"I told him."

"Well?"

"He wasn't enjoying himself caving on the land of the person concerned. There's a difference."

"I suppose there is. Look at the time! They'll be furious with us."

Cynthia turned away from the window. The dusk was falling fast, and there were some lights in the windows of the *Schloss*. "Not unless the beer runs out. But we might as well go down. I'm quite hungry."

Heather slipped her arm through Cynthia's. "You do think he's nice, though, don't you?"

"Who?"

"Albrecht."

"Of course. He would make some lucky girl a very good father."

"Darling! It's just that he's mature."

Before going to bed, Cynthia and Henry went for a walk. The moon was approaching the full. There were a few high clouds in the sky, but for the most part the moon sailed against a backdrop of stars. They walked down the hill toward the bridge that spanned the river and carried the road on in the direction of Brück-an-der-Mur.

At the bridge they rested, leaning on the worn wooden rail and watching the race of the moonlit Frohn. There was no traffic on the road. It was very peaceful.

"You were wrong about the weather," Cynthia said.

Henry nodded silently. After a pause, he said, "It's a lovely night. I'm surprised the Allens didn't want to take a walk."

"Heather wants her back rubbed. She wore herself out playing tennis today."

"I gathered that. You had a good time?"

"Very pleasant."

36

"What was all this about skeletons? She talks so fast I
can't understand her half the time."

This was the natural moment to tell Henry about it—
lightly, for their joint amusement. The excuse she had
given to Heather seemed very lame in retrospect; there
was no reason why telling Henry of so trivial a thing
should affect his studying the Frohnberg caves. It would
be as the other incidents in the past had been: she would
describe it, with casual humor, and they would both laugh.
It would be one more reinforcement of the ease and intimacy that made up their married life. Of course she must
tell Henry.

But the effort to frame a casual description was self-de-
structive. The words would not come naturally, and the
thought of expressing them in a clumsy or stilted manner
was terrifying. She was suddenly aware that the solid
ground of their mutual understanding, so taken for
granted, could be made to crack.

Striving to keep her voice calm and flat, she said, "Only
that Albrecht showed me the family vaults. All the bones
were scattered during the Occupation. Skulls and cross-
bones lying all over the floor.".

"Hasn't he had them sorted out and put back?"

"He said he's leaving that till last."

Henry said ruminatively, "An odd cove."

"Yes. I suppose so."

She had the impression she might be blushing and, although it was unlikely that it would show in the moonlight, she turned her face away from Henry. There was
reason enough, she felt, both for the blushing and the
turning away. Somehow, in a few hours, she had become a
different woman—and the kind that, in the past, she had
tolerantly despised. First in confiding in Heather, and then
in not confiding in Henry; the importance of the change
was magnified rather than depreciated by the smallness of
the incident.

It was the irrevocability that distressed her most: the
way in which, from one moment to another, ordinary reti-
cence had changed to concealment. There was no way out.
If she were now suddenly to start telling Henry about it,
she could only do so in a manner absurdly portentous and
one which, simply by being something entirely new, would
shake their relationship out of its normal ease into some
unforeseeable pattern. The obvious question for Henry to
ask would be: Why make heavy weather of it? If he did

37

ask it, she had no answer; but he might refrain from asking it, and that would be worse.

Henry was staring down at the tumbling river. "Just as well the climate has taken a turn for the better. A few more storms and it might have been too risky to go into the caves."

"Why? They're high and dry enough, aren't they?"

"In the winter floods there comes a time, apparently, when the river rises a foot in an hour. It must be something to do with a reservoir's overflowing inside the mountain. A rise of a foot down here means that the water is up to the roof in the exit tunnel. It wouldn't be much fun finding oneself trapped in there and having to wait till the river went down before one could get out."

Cynthia shivered. "No. How did you get on today?"

"Tolerably well. I gave myself a break from the paintings in the afternoon and had a look farther down. There has been a major fault somewhere. I had to clear a lot of rubble from one of the tunnels, and the passage beside the river is in a very sensitive condition—cracks in the side wall in several places."

"Don't go down there."

He put a reassuring arm across her shoulders. "You know me, Sinner. I never was the reckless type, and as I get older I get more careful. It's perfectly all right as long as one uses elementary discretion. I'm taking some equipment along into the next grotto. I shall have the paintings finished by the end of the week, and then I can do a little more exploration. There's air blowing through that crack in the far wall, and I'm pretty confident it can be opened up."

"I wish you wouldn't go any farther on your own."

"I shan't try anything that isn't absolutely in the bag. No downward corkscrews through wet chimneys. But this may be our last year here, and I want to have a scout around before I abandon it. There's probably a lake of sorts not far in, to account for the rapid rise in flood levels. I lugged the dinghy up there today."

"Our last year?"

"If I write up the painted cave, others are bound to move in. Look at the number who go to Liedl, and the Liedl caves haven't any paintings. I don't fancy forcing my way in through a mob of tourists and fellow cavers. And besides . . ."

"Besides what?"

38

"I've been imposing on you too long, old girl. The next five years we'll go for the kind of holiday you want."

"Don't be silly. You know I've loved coming to Frohnberg."

"Perhaps—but you wouldn't have come if it hadn't been for pandering to me and my cave obsession, would you? We ought not to get into the habit of going to the same place for holidays every year. We're not as middle-aged as all that. How about Venice?"

"There aren't any caves in Venice."

"There are some within reach. No, I think I'm cured of caves. Unless one is a Casteret, it's a young man's sport. As far as I'm concerned, the thrill diminishes and the discomfort increases. I've had Frohnberg to myself for five years, and I can't work up any enthusiasm for the idea of looking for another. I can retire on the strength of my footnote to speleology."

"We'll see." Cynthia nuzzled her head sideways against his chest. The distress she had felt earlier was forgotten in realizing again the security and strength of the things that tied her to Henry. She had been silly, both in talking to Heather as she had done, and in not telling Henry, but the whole business was quite unimportant when viewed against the background of her marriage.

"At any rate," Henry said, "you're not short of companionship this year, are you? Heather and Peter, and Albrecht. Tennis at the *Schloss*. Not to mention skeletons."

She laughed. "Blue-blooded skeletons, at that!"

The following morning there was a message from the *Schloss*. It was necessary for the Graf to be in the harvest fields during the early part of the day; but he hoped they would nevertheless entertain themselves at the *Schloss* and do him the honor of lunching with him there.

Cynthia and Peter tired of swimming before Heather did. They changed into clothes and then sat in deck chairs on the edge of the pool, watching her enthusiastic cavortings. She went prowling, mermaidlike, along the bottom of the pool, and popped up out of the water in front of them, releasing her pent-up breath with a great snorting gasp.

Peter called to her, "You're overdoing it. You'll be getting muscle-bound again."

She shook drops from her head. "Different muscles. Anyway, you can rub some more liniment in!"

Their smiles joined in reminiscence. Peter said, "I think you've had enough."

39

"Perhaps I have." She heaved herself up over the edge and sprawled on the boards beside them. "I think I have. Fix me up a chair while I change."

Peter stretched himself. "Time enough when you have changed." He tried, without success, to avoid the water she shook at him. "And you'd better clear off before I throw you in again."

They looked after her as she went into the pavilion.

Peter said, with unmistakable pride, "She's never learned the meaning of moderation. She always overdoes things."

"How long have you known each other?" Cynthia asked.

"About six months. It was a terribly suburban business —we met at a Tennis Club dance."

Cynthia was aware of an unusual feeling of curiosity in herself; in someone else she would have regarded it as a morbid one. She said, "And how long did you take to propose?"

Apologetically and with some reluctance Peter said, "Just under a month." He hesitated. "I'd always known the kind of girl I wanted to marry. Heather was that kind, so there didn't seem any point in wasting time."

"She's very nice," Cynthia said. "You're very lucky."

"Yes." He said it with great simplicity. Cynthia thought of what Albrecht had said the previous day. "They move through a world that transcends the world." A charming spectacle to watch, but perhaps a dangerous one: one might come to envy them their world, even while recognizing its transience and unreality.

She broke the train of thought abruptly. Now she was being silly. Good Heavens, she was a happily married woman, in the latter half of her thirties, with no serious problems and no unfulfilled desires. How could she possibly envy a young couple with all their problems before them, all the adjustments still to make?

Heather bore down on them from the pavilion. "I've been quick, haven't I?" She was still combing her wet hair back. "Peter, you beast, what about my chair?"

Peter uncurled himself and stood up. "I've been keeping it warm for you. I'll go and get another."

Heather flopped beside Cynthia with a grunt of relief. "I think I did stay in too long. Now I feel deliciously weak in the legs."

"You're certainly a glutton," Cynthia said, "for physical exercise."

"Yes, isn't it hideous? I was just like that at school. In theory the only thing I wanted to be was one of those pale, interesting girls, riddled with elegance and constipation. But I found myself captain of the netball team, captain of the lacrosse team, captain of tennis, and opening bat in the cricket team. I just couldn't resist running and jumping and making an ass of myself."

"All very healthy."

"Horribly," Heather agreed. "But I thought I'd got over it. I really must put my foot down with myself for the rest of our time here."

"Why?"

"I daren't go back home complaining of physical fatigue. I've got two younger brothers, with the filthiest kind of late-adolescent minds, and no scruples about expressing them."

Peter came out with another chair and set it up beside them.

"Albrecht's on his way," he said.

"How do you know?"

"Didn't you hear his car drive up? I suppose the pavilion cuts the sound off from this side."

Cynthia said, "He's early. I got the impression he would be out in the fields all morning."

"There must be something about our company," Heather said, "that attracts him."

Cynthia glanced at them sharply. Heather was looking at Peter with a small grin, and he was returning it broadly. There could be no doubt that Heather had confided the story about Albrecht to Peter. She saw now that it would not have been reasonable to expect anything else. She had not told Henry, but Heather had told Peter. That left Henry as the odd man out—in more senses than one, the man in the dark.

He would, she knew, be as indifferent to that as to the fact of Albrecht's having tried to kiss her. Even her own failure to tell him what she had told such a casual acquaintance as Heather—and that was the real betrayal—would rouse him to no more than concern for her wellbeing. There was no reason to worry about Henry.

Her irritation with the Allens was a different thing. Although she could not logically blame Heather for taking such a titbit of gossip to bed with her, she was annoyed at the picture it evoked—of the pair of them, smiling together at the thought of the—to them—middle-aged woman being wooed by the Austrian count while her husband

41

went cave exploring. The crux of the annoyance was seeing herself as they, in the full tide of their passion, would see her: a woman long settled into the routine of marriage, primly shocked by the advances of a yet older man.

Albrecht came out of the pavilion and walked down the veranda steps. He smiled at them easily.

"Good morning! You have all enjoyed your swimming, I hope."

"First class," Peter said. "Are you going to have a dip yourself?"

"Not now. I have been swimming already, in the early morning."

Peter's left hand hung down in the gap between his chair and Heather's. Cynthia, glancing in that direction, saw Heather's hand groping toward it as she smiled up at Albrecht. Her fingers touched it, the tips brushing across the newly licensed exciting flesh. Swiftly his hand opened, clawed down, grasped hers. Like small eager animals the two hands caught and released, twined and intertwined.

"Is the harvest going well?" Heather asked.

"If the sunshine lasts, it will." Albrecht turned toward Cynthia. "And Henry—he is still in his cave? Must he spend so much time there while the sun shines?"

The little animal that was Heather's hand caught at its larger playmate in simulated clawing fury. Peter still smiled. His hand was suddenly free and had hers in the trap of palm and fingers. He squeezed. She gave an involuntary squeak, and the captor released its prey.

Cynthia said, "He likes it down there. It needn't stop the rest of us from making hay."

"Making hay?"

"An old English proverb. Make hay while the sun shines—have a good time, while you can."

Her own voice sounded a little strange, but not unpleasantly so. She was aware of its provocativeness; a sidelong glance in Heather's direction showed that others were, too.

Albrecht said soberly, "The proverbs of many tongues, of many countries, have such a thought. But I had not guessed it would be found in England."

She said, "I thought it was your own guiding principle."

"Yes. It is."

"You seem to take your principles rather too seriously."

He saw that she was mocking him, and he smiled. "When one's principle is not to be serious, can one take it

42

too seriously? A German might, of course. The German is always most earnest about the trivial."

"But you are Austrian."

"God be thanked. There is always something worse that one might be. And now, if you have had enough of swimming for this morning, shall we go to the house and have a drink before luncheon?"

Cynthia walked with Albrecht, ahead of the Allens. She talked to him animatedly all the way, and once or twice rested her hand lightly on his arm. It was all, once she had committed herself, rather amusing.

4.

THE TWO COUPLES moved around the room to the strains of a waltz. The floor, with the carpets rolled to one side, was polished parquet. Albrecht watched them, standing by a bench seat under the main window. There were no lights on, and the room was full of the summer dusk.

The music ended, giving way to an announcement in German. Heather and Peter stood together, hands clasped, waiting for the next number.

Henry led Cynthia toward Albrecht. "A fox trot and a waltz," he said. "I've done my duty."

Cynthia asked, "Are you sure you don't want to dance, Albrecht?"

"If you wish a partner, I should be honored. But I have not danced for many years."

"I'll spare your weary bones," she said. "It will spare my own, too." She sat down in the window seat as the music started up again. "I suppose those two would dance all night. There's something frighteningly indestructible about the young."

"They have much love for each other," Albrecht observed.

Cynthia corrected him. "The illusion of much love, surely?"

"To use language is to express oneself in shorthand. We say faith, hope, love. To say illusion of faith, illusion of hope, illusion of love, tells no more, and describes the

43

same things. It would only be important if those things somewhere, in some manner, were real."

"Are you quite sure they're not?"

"No. I am not quite sure that Josef Stalin is not a saint in heaven. But if he is, then I know nothing of heaven. It is the same with love."

"Do you believe in heaven?"

Albrecht smiled. "I believe in the illusion of heaven. It is a good thing. I have seen it keep life in a man who must otherwise have died of sickness and despair."

"That was not you?"

"No. Another man."

"What kept life in you, Albrecht? After you had given up the hope of having your children inherit Frohnberg?"

Albrecht said, "The greatest illusion of all, I think. Pride. To die, as it seemed to me then, was to surrender finally to the Russians. I was right, perhaps, but only pride could make it matter."

"If everything is an illusion, surely nothing matters."

"The world around us is real, I think. It is only our thoughts about it that have no meaning. But you are right, of course. If I am a prisoner of the Russians again, I shall have more sense."

Henry said, "Not the happiest of thoughts. Albrecht, you are being extremely good to us, having us here in your house so much."

"No, I am not. You are all more than welcome."

"I don't know how Joachim is going to take it. We only seem to be at the inn to sleep."

"Joachim will not mind. You can be assured of that."

"Is there any chance of your coming to England?" Cynthia asked. "We can't offer you hospitality of this magnificence, but we should be very glad to have you stay with us."

Albrecht's eyes rested on the dancing couple. He said slowly, "I do not think that I shall see England." He turned his eyes toward Cynthia. "But thank you. You are very kind."

The music stopped, and this time the German announcement was followed by an interval signal. Heather and Peter walked off the floor to join the others. Albrecht went over to the radio to switch it off.

"What's all this about everything being an illusion?" Peter asked.

"Cynthia and Albrecht philosophizing," Henry said. "Miles over my head."

"Jolly comfortable illusion," Peter commented, his gaze ranging round the room.

Albrecht had come back. "Ah, you did not hear it all. I did not say that these things around us were an illusion."

"Oh, no, please!" Heather said. "It always gives me a headache to hear people talking about philosophy. It makes me think I'm back at school. We did philosophy in the upper sixth, and I never understood a word of it."

Albrecht smiled. "We must protect you from thinking you are back at school. What could be worse?"

They played bridge after dinner, taking turns to sit a rubber out. For the third rubber, Cynthia and Henry faced Heather and Peter. The French windows were open to the terrace; they could see Albrecht standing in the moonlight, smoking a pipe. After the first trick, Cynthia went out to join him.

As she approached, Albrecht knocked his pipe out against the stone. He did it gently—it was a meerschaum —and dropped the empty pipe in his pocket.

Cynthia chided him. "That's very wasteful. It could only have been half smoked."

"It makes nothing. You are dummy?"

She nodded. "I wanted some fresh air and moonlight. A turn up and down the terrace."

"I will walk with you, if I may."

She could imagine Heather glancing out to see their figures gone from the patch of terrace beyond the windows. The thought amused her. She drew herself up a little as she walked beside Albrecht, feeling herself tense into physical pleasure as a small breeze blew her clothes against her body. She breathed in deeply, conscious of her well-being. It was years since she had been aware of herself as young, and rich with life. The breath left her with an involuntary sigh. Albrecht bent his head toward her.

"Nothing," she said. "It's a wonderful night, isn't it?"

"Most wonderful."

They came to the end of the terrace, and she rested her arms on the stone balustrade. Through the scattered trees, it was possible to see the bright Frohn, and the village rising in terraces above it, the windows of the houses warm with light from within.

She said, "Fifty years ago, it must have looked no different, except that the lights from the windows would have been even softer and warmer."

"A hundred years," Albrecht said. "Two hundred."

45

"Fifty is enough. Nothing changed before then." She hesitated. "Before, Albrecht," she asked, "were you a Nazi?"

He shook his head gravely. "Not a Nazi. A Fascist."

"Was there any difference?"

"I have no idea. But we Austrian Fascists regarded the Nazis as underbred."

"I suppose the Russians knew about this?"

"Not at first. But they learned of it."

"It's rather amazing that they let you go at all, isn't it?"

"Yes. Perhaps they thought a returning Fascist might embarrass the government. They had overlooked that I was no more than a junior Fascist."

She looked at the profile of his face in the moonlight; at that moment the deeply drawn lines seemed to be smoothed out. It was the face of a young man.

She asked impulsively, "How old are you. Albrecht?"

He turned to her with a slight smile. "On my last birthday I was thirty-six."

She said in surprise, "Then—you're younger than I am!"

"Do years count? You are a young woman; and I, as you see, am an old man."

"Poor Albrecht."

"No. I am very lucky. I have everything I want—youth is something I do not want."

"But what do you want? Only pleasure?"

He paused—a long pause. Looking at him, she saw his gaze fixed outward on the river and the distant star-rimmed hills.

"I want to be sure," he said at last, "that there is nothing I want."

She laughed. "How long will it take you to find that out?"

"I have given myself a time limit. There would be no point in going on hunting, back and forth over the same ground, forever."

"A time limit? How long?"

"It doesn't matter." He turned away from the hills. "I think it is time that we began to walk back. The hand will be almost finished."

Cynthia turned also, letting her shoulder rest against the inside of his arm. He gave no sign of noticing it, but walked at her side along the terrace in the direction of the open lighted windows.

46

She asked, "Do you always give yourself a time limit and then abandon things that are unfinished?"

"No. You have not understood."

"I'm sorry."

"It is my fault. It is the kind of thing which it gives no profit to talk of. You must forgive me for speaking in absurd riddles. We each make our own decisions and cannot hope to justify them to others; nor should we try to do so."

"I still don't understand. Surely no one can come to decisions without considering other people as well as oneself? One can't be separate."

"Gracious lady, one is. We are here. Our talk must end now, in case it is thought to be philosophy."

He led her through the French windows into the room. Henry was making the last trick. He swept the cards up and stacked them with the others. Then he looked up at Cynthia.

"Five hearts made," he observed.

Cynthia said to the others, "I have a good and patient husband. My bidding at bridge is the one thing he reproaches me with."

Heather said, "Darling, you're fearfully lucky. My horror reproaches me with everything."

"Including," Peter said cheerfully, "your bidding at bridge. I vote we throw the women out and play poker."

Cynthia tried not to laugh at the sight of Heather on a horse. Riding, clearly, was one sport at which she was never likely to excel. She clung to the reins of the chestnut mare Albrecht had provided and defied all his patient attempts to put her at her ease.

Peter had gone off to a good fishing place Albrecht had recommended, down river from the *Schloss*. Henry, as usual, was caving. Albrecht had escorted the two women to the stables. Cynthia had trotted around the dapple-gray that he had provided for her, and returned to watch his coaching of Heather. It was not progressing far.

"Perhaps I may show you again," Albrecht said.

"Anything for a break," Heather said.

She slid off the horse in an ungainly fashion. Albrecht put his foot in the stirrup and swung himself into the saddle she had vacated. He walked, trotted, and maneuvered the horse in a brilliant display of dressage.

"Doesn't that look wonderful?" Heather sighed. "And

47

it's the very same horse. You wouldn't believe it, would you?"

He had trotted the chestnut perhaps a hundred yards from the stables and was swinging her around to come back. Cynthia mounted the dapple-gray and rode him in that direction. She passed Albrecht at a gallop, laughing, her hair streaming behind her, and continued on into the depths of the park.

She did not look back, but after a few minutes heard the noise of following hoofs. Albrecht came abreast of her and eased his horse to keep pace.

He called, "You must be careful of galloping in the park. There are branches which might cause you to fall off if you do not know where they are."

"I've ridden in woods before."

"You ride very well. You have learned as a child?"

"Yes."

He pulled to the right where trees ahead of them thickened into a clump, and she followed him obediently. The physical delight of the gallop was the only thing of which she was conscious, or wanted to be conscious. She did not look at Albrecht. The male presence riding beside her was part of the delight, but to personalize it would mean admitting questions, doubts—even guilts. She could remember a ride over the moors, when she was eighteen, in just such brilliant weather, with a young man whose name was beyond recall; in fact, everything about him was lost except the memory of his presence. It was as though she remembered the pure essentials of the experience itself—of riding through sunshine, her womanhood heightened by the man silent at her side, of being eighteen.

At the far end of the park there was a lake. Albrecht checked the chestnut, and Cynthia followed suit. They reined up a few feet from the water's edge. She still avoided looking at him, staring instead out over the lake's calm waters. She supposed that the silence would have to be broken, but she longed, almost with desperation, for it to continue.

They sat their horses. Albrecht said nothing. It was Cynthia herself who finally spoke.

"We'd better be getting back, I suppose. Heather will think we've gone mad."

He did not answer. She turned her head to look at him and found his eyes fixed on her, calmly and gently appraising. The blood burned in her cheeks.

"Are you ready to go back?" she asked.

48

"It is strange," he said.

"What is?"

"That you are English."

"Why?"

"I know little of English women. Before the war I was too young to know them, and since then I have not met them, of course. There are the conventions, naturally— one knows what one should expect of an Englishwoman, as of a German or a French."

"I'm surprised that you put trust in conventions of that kind."

"That is what is strange. At first, you and Heather both seemed the conventional Englishwoman—you especially. And, with Heather, to know her is to find her more and more of the pattern of expectation. But with you it is not so."

"Isn't it?"

"No. It is—" He broke off, hesitating. "I think you are English enough to dislike extravagances of speech. But it is as though you were a flower, coming to bloom in our Austrian sunshine."

She said awkwardly, "Thank you."

He smiled. "Yes, that is English! Shall we return now?" As they moved off, he added, "My horse a thing of wings, myself a god."

"I beg your pardon?"

"Do you not know it?" She shook her head. "It is from one of your English poems. It tells of a man who rides on St. Valentine's Day, and sees everywhere the face of his beloved."

Their horses trotted back through the trees. Ahead, in the distance, she could see the square elegance of the *Schloss*.

" 'Today, all day, I rode upon the down,' " she quoted softly.

"Yes. Then you do know it?"

"No. Someone recited it to me once—a long time ago."

"It is a poem of great beauty. I am very fond of English poetry."

"I'm afraid I don't know much poetry."

They rode the rest of the way in renewed silence. Heather was sitting on a tree trunk that had been felled not far from the stables. They dismounted beside her, and Albrecht gestured toward his horse.

"Perhaps you wish to practice once more?"

Heather said emphatically, "No fear. Seeing you two

49

gallop off like that has taken all the stuffing out of me. I've done enough riding for one day."

"Not even to walk her about?"

"Not even if she gets down on her knees and crawls. I think I'll go and pester Peter at his fishing. It will be a pleasure to walk."

Cynthia said, "We'll come along with you."

"I thought you would want to go on riding together."

Cynthia glanced at Albrecht; his eyes, fixed on her, were curious. She said to Heather, "I'd rather walk down with you and find Peter, if you have no objection."

Heather surveyed them, blandly innocent. "None at all."

Albrecht nodded. "We will all walk there. I will just get Heinrich to see to the horses."

They played a couple of sets of tennis in the afternoon, but the heat was too much even for Heather's enthusiasm, and they took to the pool instead. Afterwards they lay on the side, sun-bathing. Peter, drowsy and doped with sun-light, would have fallen asleep, were it not that Heather continually tormented him into wakefulness, prodding, pinching and tickling.

At last he rolled over and faced her. "Go away. Find something to occupy yourself with."

"I've got something, darling."

"My last warning. Next thing, I heave you in the pool."

Heather giggled. "Lovely!" She stretched out a bare foot and prodded his stomach with it. "Go ahead."

"No. If I did, you would probably come to the side and splash water over me. In any case, it's too hot for any kind of exertion."

"You mean you're too lazy." Heather stretched herself luxuriously. "Gosh, it is hot, though." She looked across at where Cynthia lay, face down and motionless. "Lucky old Henry in his nice cool caves."

There was no comment from the others. Peter rolled over again. Suddenly Heather sat upright. "Let's go and surprise him!"

Peter's muted voice said, "Yes. You go."

"No, all of us. Just the thing on an afternoon as hot as this. Come on."

"Wild Arabian steeds couldn't drag me," Peter commented.

"Don't be silly. We must see the caves sometime."

"In a short while," Albrecht said, "there will be tea."

"It's too hot for afternoon tea, anyway. We could wear our costumes for getting across the river."

50

"The river is sharply cold, even at this season of year."

"We all need cooling off."

Albrecht parked the car beside the road and unlocked the gate. Following in single file along the ledge, they passed from brightness and heat into the cave's cool darkness. Albrecht shone his torch ahead onto the pile of rubble that blocked the way.

"It is better to wade from here," he said.

Cynthia drew back from the prospect of the darkly teeming water.

She said, "This is absurd. I'm not going to walk through that on a harebrained notion of Heather's. I'll go back and wait outside for you."

Albrecht slipped off the ledge into the Frohn. The light from his torch was directed into the cave; the light that filtered in from the entrance was only enough to show him as a shadowy outline.

He said, "You do not need to go in the water. I will carry you, as I did before."

Heather's voice, amused, said, "You mustn't pass that up, darling."

"And you," Peter said to Heather, "can carry me."

Cynthia could just see Albrecht's arms, stretched out to receive her. She reached down toward them and put her own arms about his neck. He held her with one arm—the one carrying the torch—under her knees, and the other supporting her back. Both men were wearing bathing trunks. The dry warmth of his flesh tightened against her own.

Heather said, "Here goes for the plunge!" There was a splash as she entered the water, followed by a series of high-pitched little shrieks.

She cried, "Ooh, it's freezing!"

"Stand still," Peter said, "so that I can climb on your back."

"Give me your hand, then," Heather said. There was a small scuffle, and then another splash. They heard her shriek. "Got you! If there's any climbing on backs to do, I'll do it."

Albrecht turned his head. He said sternly, "Please. There must not be careless movements or any loud noises. There has been a land fault, and the wall is not safe. We must all go warily."

"We'll be good," Heather said.

"But for God's sake," Peter added, "let's get cracking.

It's all right for Heather, and as far as I know you may be constructed of solid brass, but this monkey's a tender plant."

Heather began to laugh and then, remembering Albrecht's warning, moderated her laughter. She said in a penetrating whisper, "Darling, I'm just as concerned for you as if it were myself. But you must be standing in a hole. Where I am, it's not much above the knees."

The strange echoing quality of voices underground and the embracing darkness gave Cynthia a dreamlike feeling. The voices of Heather and Peter, the splash of their progress upstream, the low roar of the river itself, were all distant and unreal impressions, emphasizing the one impression that was close and real—almost overpoweringly real —the touch of Albrecht's flesh against her own.

His voice sounded against her ear. "Are you comfortable?"

"Yes."

The monosyllable, jerked out of her, was a lie. With each step Albrecht took forward, comfort increasingly gave way to tension. It was a double tension, requiring a double discipline. Not only was there the temptation to make some voluntary action—to tighten her fingers still further against the flesh on which they rested, to brush her lips against the face that was no more than inches from her own—but there was also the growing fear that her body would betray her against her desperately summoned will, that the fingers would tighten and clutch of their own volition, her whole body begin to shiver from the physical pleasure that mounted in it. She strove to force her mind away from her body altogether and at the same time to blanket the body's joy by the cold exercise of will.

The time between Albrecht's taking her in his arms and their reaching the entrance to the first cavern was an immeasurable one. He lifted her forward and she clutched the hard bare rock in a fierceness that gave her some relief. She pulled herself through the hole and stood upright. She was shivering now, violently and uncontrollably.

The others came through after her. Heather touched her arm.

"Cyn, you're quivering like a blancmange!"

She said, keeping her voice flat, "It's cold in here—after the sunshine outside."

"You should have taken the plunge back there," Heather said cheerfully. "Anything seems warm after that river."

52

Peter was the last to come through. He looked around as Albrecht flashed the torch in a slow arc.

"What?" he asked. "No stalactites—no prehistoric monsters? Just a hole in the ground."

"There are stalactites in the next cave," Albrecht said. He adjusted the beam of his torch to throw a more diffuse light. "We must climb up that slope at the end."

"We could," Peter observed, "have been lying by the pool, consolidating our tans, had I not, in a fit of madness, married a woman who's permanently crackers. Or else drinking tea, which I could do with at the moment."

"Shut up," Heather told him. "I think this is great fun. Except that canvas shoes don't strike me as the best kind of footwear for it, especially when soaked."

They wriggled through into the grotto, and Albrecht, readjusting the torch beam, traced the outline of its walls. He led them over to the stalactite palisade.

"These are the stalactites," he explained.

"Not up to Wookey," Peter said, "and going into Wookey doesn't involve risk of life and limb."

"Darling," Heather said, "which limb was it you were risking?" She put her hand out and caressed the nearest stalactite with her fingers. "There's something awfully thrilling about this. I'm beginning to understand what Henry sees in it. How do we get to where Henry is?"

"It is more difficult still," Albrecht told her. "Are you certain you wish to go farther?"

"Yes, of course. Lead the way."

Cynthia went first again through the chimney. She could hear Heather noisily scrabbling along behind her. The light at the other end of the chimney brightened. By the time she had heaved herself through into the painted cave, Henry was standing there with the acetylene lamp, waiting to help her to her feet.

He said, "I didn't expect visitors. Aren't you cold in just a bathing costume?"

"Heather's idea," Cynthia said. "You'd better give her a hand up."

The others scrambled through in turn. Albrecht said, "I hope we do not interrupt you. But of course we do."

"That's all right. I've just about finished for the day. What's it like outside?"

"Very hot. That is what made Heather want to come."

Heather had taken the torch from Albrecht and was prowling about the cave. She called back to them, "Is this one of the famous paintings?"

53

Henry and Albrecht started to speak together. Albrecht stopped, and let Henry go on. "You must not call out like that, Heather. There's a fault that runs all the way through here. Only talk in a low voice, and be careful how you walk."

Heather said cheerfully, "O.K. Sorry. Peter, come and have a look at the paintings."

Henry said to Peter, "Try to impress on her how important it is not to disturb anything."

"I'll throttle her," Peter said obligingly, "if she doesn't behave herself."

They all crossed to where Heather was standing. She was looking at the painted bison with a critical air. "It looks like something of Picasso's, doesn't it? What's made all the holes in it?"

"Spears or arrows," Henry said. "We imagine the cave men must have thrown them at the paintings; a lot of them look like that."

"That's what I've always wanted to do myself," Peter said, "but I never had the nerve. What was the bloke who painted them doing while his fellow cave men went in for this boisterous form of criticism?"

"They probably shot him full of holes before they got started on the paintings," Heather suggested. "They had bags of go in those days."

Albrecht said, "Henry has earlier explained to us that the throwing was to work magic. If your arrow pierced the painting of the bison, then in the hunt you might strike down the beast itself, and so bring food to the tribe."

"Why not make a clay model and stick pins in it?" Heather asked. "I did that on a French teacher once."

Peter asked her, "What happened?"

"She left at the end of term to get married." Heather added with satisfaction, "To an Englishman. Serves her right."

"There are clay models in some caves," Henry said. "The natives in these parts seem to have thought that paintings were good enough."

"Show me the rest," Heather said. "Are there any of dinosaurs and ptero-what's-its?"

"I've already made the tour," Cynthia said. "I'll wait here till you come back."

Heather and Peter went off with Henry. Henry said, "There would be something wrong if there were. The big lizards were extinct long before man came on the scene."

54

Henry was carrying the acetylene lamp, which was the only light in the cave. The pool of soft light retreated from Cynthia and Albrecht, leaving them in darkness.

Albrecht asked, "Do you want me to put on the torch?"

She tried to keep the strain out of her voice. "No. I don't mind the dark."

"But you did not wish to come here?" She did not answer. The others were at the far end of the cavern; they could hear the indistinguishable murmur of Henry's voice explaining something. "She is a very headstrong girl, is she not?"

Cynthia said bitterly, "She can afford to be."

"Why do you say that?" —

Why indeed? Cynthia thought. Because there is nothing to stop her taking what she wants; while I am only just beginning to learn what it is to want something—with a kind of wanting that turns my placid happy life upside down—and to know that I can't have it. She did not speak now, because she did not dare to.

Albrecht's hand touched her arm. His hand opened; the fingers moved with deliberation down to her wrist and held it for a moment. Then, releasing the wrist, the hand clasped on her own.

He said softly, "Cynthia!"

Her eyes were closed. She opened her mouth, taking in a deep breath of the cave's moist air. She drew the whole of her lower lip in between her teeth, and knew the relief of pain as her teeth tightened on her flesh.

This was the critical moment. Her hand lay, unmoving, within Albrecht's. In all her life, she had never wanted anything more than she wanted now to return the pressure of his fingers. If she did so, by no more than a tremor, the gates would go down, and there would be no resisting the flood that must sweep her away. But if, somehow, she could summon the last strength of her cringing will to reject him, then surely she was safe. He would not make a third advance, because she would not again be such a fool as to let Heather provoke her into encouraging him.

She pleaded with herself: Just this, and then it's easy. For the rest of the week, she could stay always in the presence of the Allens. After that, Henry would be willing to move on for the rest of the fortnight, if she asked him. There would be no difficulty about that. All that was needed was now, at this moment, the power to say no to her own desires.

At the other end of the cave, Heather began to laugh

55

about something and then checked herself. As she did, Cynthia pulled her hand free from Albrecht's. She moved a pace or two away from him. Her success strengthened her for more. She said in a steady voice, "We might as well go and see what's amusing Heather. It's as sensible as standing here in the dark waiting for them. Put the torch on, so that we can see where we're going."

He obeyed her without a word, and they made their way forward and up the slope over the rubble. When she stumbled once, his hand steadied her, but that was all.

She said, "Thank you."

She was conscious of overwhelming relief, realizing how close she had come to making a fool of herself. Passion had been stilled with the single movement that withdrew her hand from Albrecht's. It was frightening that a level-headed, happily married woman could let herself be dragged, almost without resistance, to the very brink of a sordid *affaire;* but at the same time it was reassuring that one could retrieve oneself from that brink by an act of will.

It could have happened to me, she thought—that was something I didn't know about myself. But, knowing it, I'm safe. It can't happen again.

Peter, as they approached, tripped over a stone and almost fell.

"Blast!" he said. "At least that sort of thing never happens in the National Gallery."

"You are dull," Heather said. "I think it's much more exciting looking at pictures this way. What's that? Isn't it a hand? What did they want to paint hands for? They didn't eat them, did they?"

Henry said, "It's not a painting. They're quite common. It's the actual impression of a hand. There are several others farther along."

"You mean they dipped their hands in the paint pot, and then stuck them on the wall? What on earth did they do that for?"

"Look at it closely," Henry said.

Peter craned his neck. "It's a couple of fingers light," he announced. "Little finger and third."

"As far as we know," Henry said, "they chopped their fingers off as a kind of sacrifice. Perhaps when one of the family died, or the chief of the tribe. Or perhaps to ward off evil spirits when the hunting was bad, or the stream dried up. It's all guessing, of course, but most of the paint hands you find are mutilated." He directed the light far-

56

ther along the wall. "There's a beauty. All four fingers gone, and the top of his thumb. After they had wielded the flint chopper, they would come up here and record the sacrifice for posterity. I'll bet that old boy was proud of himself."

"And here we are—" Peter said— "posterity. Well, I'm impressed."

Heather said, "Would you chop your little finger off if I died, sweetie?" .

Peter whispered something in her ear, and she giggled.

"Peter! And I can just see you doing it, too! You'd have a wonderful time as a widower."

Henry said, "The hands mark the end of the paintings. At least, I haven't found any more."

"Are there more caves?" Heather asked.

"Yes."

"With paintings?"

"No. Some nice displays of gypsum flowers, though."

"Do show us."

"Not today," Peter said firmly. "Not in these wet swimming trunks particularly. I'm expecting stalactites to start forming down my legs."

"Don't be mean," Heather said.

Henry said, "It is too late, Heather, and you would really need to be properly dressed. It's a trickier way than the climb up here."

"Can we come back another day," Heather asked, "when we've got lots of time? And in proper clothes?"

"Of course, if you want to. Give me a couple of days on my own, first. By then I might be able to clear the way a bit for you."

"I'll hold you to that," Heather said. "I think caves are thrilling. Are we going back now? Are you coming with us?"

"I might as well. I'll just shove the camera and stuff in my haversack."

They scrambled down through the chimney and across the two outer caves. At the prospect of the hole leading to the river, Heather said, "It doesn't look at all cheerful. Forget about the chopper, darling, I'll take my tribute now. You can ferry me across, as Albrecht did for Cynthia."

Peter said in a resigned voice, "I don't suppose I've got any option. But one wriggle and I drop you. Here goes."

He slid through the hole and into the water, carrying the torch which Albrecht had passed on to him. Heather

57

followed, and there was the sound of Peter's grunts of pretended exhaustion and Heather's indignant protests.

Henry said, "Do you think you could manage Cynthia on the return trip as well, Albrecht? I've got this pack and I'm anxious not to soak the camera."

"I shall be very glad to do so."

Cynthia watched the two men slide backward through the hole. Her emotions were quite untouched; the triumph she had had in the painted cave was sufficient armor, she felt, against the few minutes during which she would be in Albrecht's arms. She wriggled down, and found his arms safely holding her. He stepped away from the side, and against the distant light of the entrance she saw the others ahead of them: Peter with Heather in his arms, and Henry adjusting the pack on his shoulders.

Although they could see the others, they must themselves be invisible against the darkness of the tunnel, and in any case the others were all looking out toward the daylight. They were doubly hidden, and, with the awareness of this, desire suddenly returned, the pleasure—the pain —flowing uncontrollably to every last inch of her body. She could have wept at the folly of her own confidence, at having thought that by taking her hand from his she could make herself safe even for half an hour.

The only hope, she saw, was that he would fail to realize how it was with her—that he would not look for a second rebuff in so short a time. She concentrated on checking the trembling in her limbs, holding herself rigid and aloof. As Albrecht waded on, she knew that it was working. In a couple of minutes she would be on the ledge beyond the landslip—and it would be over.

It would be over, irrevocably . . . in less than a minute now.

She was aware that he had stopped going forward before she was fully aware of something else—that her hands were fiercely pressing behind his neck, her voice whispering brokenly against his face. They stood motionless in the dark, and the current swirled round them, pulling, pulling down.

5.

THE NEXT MORNING, at breakfast, Cynthia said to Henry, "Do you have to go today?"

Henry smeared honey on his buttered roll. "Go where?"

"To the caves."

He looked at her in mild surprise. "Don't you want me to go?"

"I thought a break might be good for you. This weather may not last. It seems a pity that you have to go down into those dark dungeons every day."

Henry meticulously restored to the top of the roll a thin trickle of honey that had escaped over the edge.

He said, "You know my passion for finishing a job off once I've started it. I'll take a break afterward."

"The weather may have broken by then."

"Well, there are two ways of looking at that. The Frohn hasn't gone down much, if at all. If I left it alone and then the rains came back, the corridor to the next grotto might be impassable."

Cynthia looked out of the window to the sunny roofs of Frohnberg; she was aware of a mingled feeling of numbness and exhilaration. In the sense of detachment this provided, she saw herself as having, by her plea, freed herself of guilt in advance; and also saw her own complacency in having done so.

Henry poured himself more coffee. He said thoughtfully, "Unless *you're* getting fed up with my being down under every day. It is a nuisance for you."

She could not look at him naturally, and so kept her eyes on the window. While she was searching her mind for the right sort of remark, he went on:

"I'm afraid I haven't given it a thought. You never complained other years, and this time there are Albrecht and the Allens. I assumed they would be entertaining you."

"They are." She turned her eyes from the window now, toward the face, at once familiar and completely strange, of her husband. She said in a flat voice, but perfectly conscious of the irony, "I was thinking of you."

59

Henry smiled. "It's true that at the present rate I shan't take much of an Austrian tan back to London."

"The important thing is that you're enjoying yourself."

"After my fashion. What were you planning to do today?"

"Nothing in particular." One of her hands shivered slightly and she pressed it down against the table. "No fixed plans."

"I could leave things over for a day, if you'd rather."

She shook her head. "No. I don't want to come between you and your passion."

Albrecht had followed what was now his usual practice of spending the early morning in the harvest fields. Cynthia found herself annoyed by this, although, as she told herself, the annoyance was irrational. In addition, it was not unmixed with relief. They had exchanged no word the previous afternoon, and she had not been alone with him since then. She had no means of gauging his feelings; nor, for that matter, her own.

After they had swum, Heather developed a whim to walk through the park. She made only a cursory attempt to persuade Peter to accompany her—he had stretched himself out on the grass near the pool, feigning sleep—but was persistent with Cynthia.

Cynthia could see the face of her watch without moving her head. It was getting near time that Albrecht might be expected to arrive. She rolled over and sat up.

"All right. But a cigarette first."

The successive days of sunshine had drawn the last dampness out of the earth, but had left it still springy and the grass deep green with sap. At first Cynthia paid small attention to Heather's chatter, listening to it only to an extent which permitted her to make the necessary interjections or responses at the necessary intervals. She was startled into giving heed by hearing the words "unfaithful" and "husband" but she had missed the context.

She asked idly, "What was that?"

"Haven't you ever thought about it?"

"About what?"

"Well—having an *affaire?*"

She said, "No." It would have been true a week ago.

"But you must have! You told me you'd had to deal with men before—when you were talking about Albrecht."

"The fact that they may have thought about it doesn't mean that I did."

60

"I wasn't talking about thinking *seriously*—just thinking. What you would feel like, if . . . Of course, you couldn't."

Cynthia smiled. "And what would you feel like?"

"Tingly-wingly, I'd like to think—butterflies up and down my spine." She sighed gustily. "But they would probably be up and down my large intestine. I should be much too scared."

"Do you regret that?"

"Goodness, no. Not if it saves me from a sordid do."

"Are they all sordid?" Cythia asked.

"Well, I suppose so. They must be. But I'd like to have better reasons for being a virginal wife."

Cynthia laughed. "You mean chaste."

"Do I? Yes, I see what you mean." She paused briefly. "There's something so dreadful about doing ordinary things because one hasn't the guts to do the others. Don't you feel like that?"

They were abreast of the turreted mausoleum. Cynthia looked in that direction. "The ordinary things are good enough for me."

"No, you don't understand—" She broke off, following Cynthia's gaze. "The scene of the crime? It's rather nice in its way, isn't it?"

"Ordinary, I should have thought."

"I wasn't talking about the building. I meant Albrecht, upping and kissing you across the bones of his forefathers. It's doing something, instead of being scared stiff of moving one foot outside the white line someone has laid down for you."

"That," Cynthia said, "is one way of looking at it, I suppose."

Heather said with regret, "It's a pity he's not the kind of handsome young count novelists write about."

"Is it?"

"Well, isn't it? I'd be madly envious, if he were."

Albrecht was sitting in a chair when they returned to the pool. He got up as they approached and made them his little courtly bow. His smile was remote and offered impartially to both of them.

Heather went and stirred Peter with her foot. "Asleep again? Wake up. I want to be amused."

"Do you wish," Albrecht asked, "to have more practice in riding?"

Heather shuddered. "I'm still sore from the last time."

61

She lifted one foot onto a chair and displayed the inside of her thigh. "Look—it's practically raw."

"The horses should be exercised," Albrecht said. "Is Peter a horseman?"

Heather put her foot down again, on the small of Peter's back. She rolled him slightly in either direction.

"Not a bit."

Albrecht looked at Cynthia, but still distantly.

"So we must exercise them," he said. "You do not mind this?"

She felt her throat constrict. "No. I enjoy riding."

Albrecht said to Heather, "You will excuse us, then?"

"Go ahead. I'll stay and watch him dreaming, and kick him when he smiles."

They walked around the side of the house toward the stables; neither spoke. The horses, Cynthia found, were already saddled; he must have given instructions for that before going out to the pool. He helped her to mount before taking the chestnut from the groom. Then, still without a word, they were cantering together through the trees.

Albrecht broke the silence as they approached the lake. "Do you jump?"

"Nothing above three feet."

He nodded and turned along the left shore of the lake. There was a low wall, marking the end of the park, and he set his horse at it. Cynthia followed without much difficulty. But the ground was rougher on the other side, and rising towards the encircling hills. Their pace dropped to a trot, and then to a walk. They came to a halt in the lee of an overhang of rock. They dismounted, and Albrecht tethered the two horses to a sapling.

The overhang provided shade from the heat of a sun near its zenith. A breeze seemed to run along the base of the rock. One could look down the slope, over the scattered tops of trees, to the *Schloss* and the river, and Frohnberg rising on the other side.

The horses were cropping. Cynthia said, "One would have to be as ignorant of such things as Heather is, to believe you would leave their exercising to the chance of an opportunity's turning up during the day."

Albrecht stood beside her, his arm almost touching her shoulder. He said, "I think you are right, perhaps."

"What if she had decided to come, after all? She's very keen on exercise."

"I did not think she would."

There was silence, lasting for perhaps a minute. At first

62

she resented the briefness of his replies and his failure to
break the silence, which seemed to show indifference. But
then, when she had the feeling that he was about to say
something, she was afraid of what he might say. She spoke
herself, quickly and unevenly.

"Don't say anything—not now. I don't want anything
like that. I only want . . ."

Their arms touched, sought, grasped. She felt the firm-
ness of his body against her own, the unexpected, bruising
hardness of his lips.

"Is it possible to speak again?"

Having finished combing her hair, Cynthia returned the
comb to Albrecht. She smiled at him. Nothing was as she
had expected—no guilt, no remorse. Perhaps they would
come later. At present there was only contentment; she
was grateful for it.

"Yes, of course. I felt you had the idea I wanted you to
say things—the sort of things people are supposed to say
at times like that—and that you were going to say them. I
couldn't bear the thought of it."

"I was going to say them, even though I knew they
would be false."

She laughed. "That's very honest of you."

"For very simple people they might not be false, because simple people think words have simple meanings.
That is not so with us, is it?"

"No."

One of the horses raised its head from the grass and
looked down the slope of trees as though watching someone. It was an entirely innocent scene, Cynthia reflected,
except that her hair had been only roughly combed back,
and she had no idea how her face looked. With all her
thought and preparation, she had forgotten to bring her
compact; it was a damning indictment, she decided, of her
possibilities as a loose woman.

The horse dropped its head, and continued to crop. She
put her hand on Albrecht's where it rested beside her, and
stroked the hard, dry skin. As she did so, she felt the first
twinge of guilt, but there was little difficulty in submerging
it in the warmth of sensual pleasure.

She said, "I suppose you were confident of seducing me
all along—even before the kiss among the bones?"

He said seriously, "No. I was not confident."

"Why not?"

"I thought you were not that kind of woman."

63

"And now you know better."

He covered her hand with his. "No. I know the same. You are not that kind of woman."

She felt guilt now; she was conscious of shame scorching her cheeks. Had Albrecht been cynical or indifferent, it would not have mattered, but his sympathy shattered her armor. She strove to keep her voice light.

"I can't think of anyone better qualified. A married woman who falls into the arms of a man she has only known two or three days—what else do you want?"

Albrecht said, "I do not think you have done this before."

She did not answer. Two white butterflies darted in fluttering chase; against the green first and then, spiraling high, against the blue—blown by the wind, on a windless day.

"Tell me," Albrecht persisted. "Am I not right?"

"Does it matter?"

"It matters that you accuse yourself too harshly. Tell me—it has not happened before?"

She looked at him reluctantly. "No."

"You see."

She shook her head. "I was never tempted before—not in that way. I can't take any credit for it."

"But do not take too much blame."

She smiled, her mouth twisting. "There's something you haven't said yet, Albrecht."

"What is that?"

"You haven't told me how much you love me." He looked at her in silence. "It's silly, isn't it—the idea of saying things like that to a person who's no more than a casual acquaintance? Or a casual mistress."

"Does it make so much difference?"

"I think it's best to see things as they are. We know what we want from each other. And I think that makes me that kind of woman, doesn't it?"

There was a pause before he replied. "It was a foolish thing for me to say. People are not kinds of women, or kinds of men. And we must learn to forgive ourselves. If we do not ask God to forgive us, then we must forgive ourselves."

"That's easy, isn't it?"

"I do not think easy."

"No, perhaps it isn't. You have to be sorry before you can be forgiven, even if you are forgiving yourself. It isn't good enough just to be ashamed."

"But if you are not sorry, then you do not need to be

64

forgiven. Shame is something that has no meaning. When the Russians, learning of my rank, gave me disgusting work to do, I was ashamed. That was in the early years. In the later years I knew it was they who should be ashamed."

"This is a different thing. I'm not being ashamed of something imposed on me by others. No one has imposed it."

"Life imposes." He smiled. "That is philosophy, which makes Heather's head ache."

She smiled in return. "Yes."

After that, they sat in silence for several minutes, only their hands moving occasionally against each other. In that silence the sense of shame gradually subsided again: the ease which they shared seemed something good and innocent; and yet it derived from the physical passion which had earlier moved them. The butterflies, she saw, were returning, hovering now, unperturbed, in a calm sky.

"We should be getting back," she said at last.

"Yes."

He made no move. She lay back against the sweetsmelling grass and stared up the face of rock which leaned over them.

She said, "Albrecht?"

"Yes."

"There was something you said—on the terrace, the night before last: about giving yourself a time limit."

"I don't remember."

"I do—very clearly. What did you mean?"

"Nothing that matters now."

"You were talking about making sure there was nothing in life you wanted. What happens when the time limit expires?"

"What should happen? Then I know I have no desires."

She raised herself to a sitting position once more. He was staring down toward the *Schloss;* his features showed their usual withdrawn melancholy, nothing more.

She asked him, "Do you owe me anything?"

He turned to her. "Very much."

"A few moments' honesty?"

He said seriously, "If that is what you wish."

"It is. I want to know what you meant."

He was silent for several seconds before he said, "I told you that often, during the time I was a prisoner, it would have been easier to die than it was to live. At first I made

65

hopes, to give me cause for living, and later I lived because of pride.

"Hope is a strange thing—I do not mean a particular hope, but hope itself; the power of hoping, as one would speak of the power of loving. I think that once it has been killed, nothing can make it live. When I came back here, to my home, I could not learn to hope again. I had money, my home still stood—there was much to live for. But nothing to hope for. All the things that were given back to me were empty and without meaning. I would have died in Russia if I had not hated them so much, and now they had set me free I had lost even that."

Cynthia said, "Why did you restore the *Schloss*, if you felt like that?"

Albrecht looked down the valley. "I came back here, to my home. The soldiers had left it in the previous year. Since then nothing had been done. The damage was all on the surface, of course—I could see that—but it is the surface of things which is most striking to us. I walked through the empty rooms and saw the broken windows, the plaster falling away from the walls, the tiles on the great stoves chipped and shattered.

"And I had found that for me life no longer had any meaning. I had fulfilled the only purpose that had been left—I had lived through my captivity and come back to Austria. To me the only question was how best to die."

Cynthia listened to the matter-of-fact voice without surprise or incredulity. What Albrecht was saying was describing him and, somehow, she felt, describing herself also.

"I had been a soldier, and a soldier thinks of a revolver in such a case; but I had none. I could have hanged myself in the empty house, but I had a horror of that kind of death. Instead, I thought of the lake. When I was a child, there had been a mystery and a fascination about it, because an uncle of mine, not many years before, had drowned himself there. Although it is shallow at the sides, it is very deep in the middle. I decided I would drown myself there."

"Can one drown oneself," Cynthia asked, "if one can swim?"

"My uncle was a skilled swimmer. He was a soldier, and for more than twenty years had lived only for soldiering. Then he had left his regiment, dishonorably, on account of a woman, and he had lost the woman. He walked

66

into the lake. Perhaps such a thing requires determination, but to live may require it even more.

"So I left the house and went through the park toward the lake. It was November, and although there had not yet been snow, the clouds were heavy with it, and it was very cold. I had the thought that if the boats had not all been destroyed it would be more comfortable to row out to the lake's center."

He smiled. "Even at such a time, one thinks of comfort. I had to pass the mausoleum, and I looked in there. I saw that the bones of the dead had been scattered and desecrated. That was something I had not expected. And while I had not minded leaving the *Schloss* itself battered and unkempt, it seemed to me that I could not leave these. It may be I was deceiving myself." His smile deepened. "It was a very cold day to drown oneself in a lake."

Cynthia said, "But you left them as they were, after all?"

"It was late in the afternoon, and I decided that on the next day I would get help to rearrange the bones in their places and then do as I had intended. But that evening I began to despise myself—not for choosing to die, but for choosing it for the wrong reason: out of weakness and tiredness and being disillusioned.

"I decided that I would live for a time—that I would go back into life, restore my home. Only after that could I leave it without the suspicion in my own mind that I was dying because I lacked the strength to live. I gave myself a year. The bones I left as they were in the mausoleum, because that should be the last thing that I would do. Then it is finished."

The August sun was warm on her bare arm. She said, "It will be cold again in November."

"Yes. The frost might come early, and I do not think it would be easy to break ice so that one might die." She saw him smiling, but this time his smile frightened her. "But I have a revolver again, and also I have one of those small glass capsules which makes it still more easy. It is all prepared."

What he had told her was something which, with a part of her mind, she had known already; it had been the image of death, above his quiet eyes, that had drawn her to him. She did not doubt his words, nor his intention. Instead she was strangely conscious of a sense of failure in herself. Behind her physical desire there had been the need to draw him back from his mortality into the world's

67

warmth. She wondered unhappily how many other women, since his return, had tasted the same bitterness of defeat.

She asked him, "Have you told anyone else of this?"

"No."

The urge to argue or plead with him was strong, but she knew the uselessness of words. She thought of "The Snow Queen"—the dagger of frost in the heart that no human love would ever melt. She moved toward him, and he took her in his arms. But the dagger was still there; her kisses could not touch it.

The garden was on the west side of the *Schloss*. It was, Albrecht had explained, an English garden, which his grandmother had had made after a visit to England at the end of the last century. It was walled with red brick, and one entered it through a narrow gate. Inside, paths rambled aimlessly between flower beds packed with an untidy profusion of flowers. There were arbors and sundials, and the whole of it was sunk below the level of the surrounding ground, so that water could be piped in from the Frohn. The water emerged, splashing, from one of the walls, and meandered downward over pink- and gold-tinged granite toward a surprisingly formal rectangular lily pond.

This evening, as they walked, the air was heavy with the scent of stock. It was as though the deepening purple sky breathed out perfume.

Heather said, "This is the kind of garden I want."

"In Croydon?" Peter asked.

"When we're very, very rich," Heather explained.

"O.K.," Peter said. "But no steps, mind. I shall want a ramp for the bath chair."

"Are not English gardens like this, then?" Albrecht asked.

Henry smiled. "A few—at large country houses."

"I was not thinking of size, but of the wall, and the many different kinds of flowers together, that is what my grandmother called English."

Heather said to Peter, in a small voice, "You shouldn't *talk* about growing old."

Peter cupped a brilliant double dahlia in his hand. "Why not? I've always looked forward to it. The only reason I took my present job is because it's got a pension geared to the cost of living."

"The English garden," Henry said, "is three parts plan-

68

tain lawn, and one part herbaceous border, surrounded by fences not quite high enough for privacy and not quite low enough to let the passer-by have a look at it. It has to be seen to be believed. You must come and see it."

Cynthia said, "It's not quite as bad as that. Henry just doesn't like gardening. That makes him feel un-English, so he attacks gardens on principle."

"And is that not thought un-English—to attack gardens?"

"Not if you do it in strong, cynical terms. That lets you qualify as an eccentric."

"I'm allergic to soil," Peter said. "It brings me out in boils."

"Darling," Heather said, "that's loathsome! You mustn't talk about yourself growing old. And you can't possibly look forward to it. It's hideous."

"Think of what they can do for you these days," Peter said. "Toupees, false teeth, contact lenses, hearing aids concealed in your left eyebrow . . . With a corset and a jar of hormone cream, I'll look as good as new. We can share the hormone cream if you like—pat it under each other's chins on Saturday nights."

"There was a man who was a prisoner with me," Albrecht said, "who made a garden. It was no more than a yard square. He managed to get flowers from somewhere —none of us knew where. When the frosts came, he covered his garden with old sacks."

"And it kept him alive?" Henry asked.

"No. It killed him. We others took the sacks for our beds; we had few blankets and it was very cold. In the morning he went out and saw that all his plants were dead. He took a chill the next day, and it became pneumonia. Within a week, he was dead."

Heather hammered her husband with her fists. "You horrible brute! I won't have you growing old."

"In that case, I shall have to die young." He grinned at her in the twilight. "Conceivably of exhaustion."

"But he couldn't have kept plants alive all winter by covering them with sacking, surely—particularly in Russia," said Henry.

"No. It was all inevitable."

Cynthia, unable to resist the impulse, put her hand onto Albrecht's; she was walking between the two men. He pressed it gently and released it. His doing so made her realize the folly of her action. She blushed—not, as she had done before on the bridge, because of what she had

69

become, but because of the risk. It was strange, she thought, that she could so easily get used to a picture of herself which a week earlier would have horrified her. She gave precise expression to her thought: she was physically infatuated with another man. It was losing its power to shock.

Heather said imperiously, "You're not to die young, either."

"Not much choice left, is there?"

"What's the moral of that sad story?" Henry asked. "That one mustn't get attached to gardens?"

"To anything. But for nearly all people it is impossible advice, and for the rest it is unnecessary—they have lost the ability to become attached, or else never had it."

"And in which category would you place yourself, Albrecht? You survived, at any rate."

Albrecht said quietly, "I think I had it once."

Heather steered Peter toward the lily pond; they stood beside it, looking down at the dim green pads of the lilies.

"I remember this," Peter said, "in the spring. You should have seen the garden—it was an absolute ruin. And this pond was empty—I think the bottom had cracked and the water had run away. Anyway, I wandered in here one afternoon, and the sight was quite astonishing."

"You tell stories shockingly badly," Heather told him affectionately. "What sight?"

"The empty pond was jam-packed with frogs mating. You've never seen such a tangle—they were three and four deep in places. Not making any movement; just clutched together as though their lives depended on it."

"Darling!" Heather said. "How lovely!"

"Yes, it was rather fascinating. But a bit unnerving, as well. Hundreds of frogs literally wrapped up in each other."

She pinched him secretly. "Why can't you be like those wise frogs?"

"What—three or four deep?"

"Oh, you horror!"

"There were a couple of the men there. It was they who drew my attention to it. They had been sent into the garden to dig a hole for something and they had their spades with them. One of them tried to prise a couple apart with the edge of his spade."

"And did he?"

"No. They wouldn't budge."

"Good for them!"

70

"So he used his spade as a knife. He got them apart in the end, but he had to cut the legs off one of them to do it."

Heather stared down into the waters of the pool, attracted and horrified. "And you let him!"

"What else could I do?"

"You were an officer—you could have stopped him."

"A junior officer can't afford to get branded as a sentimentalist. We had a cook who used to catch rats and roast them alive in a stove." She shuddered violently. "It takes all kinds to make an army."

"Stop talking about it! I hate you to talk about things like that. I think I hate you a bit anyway, for the sake of the frogs."

The others had come up beside them. Albrecht inquired, "Frogs? I have not seen any here. Before the war there were always frogs, and very noisy."

"A horrible story of Peter's," Heather said. "He's not to talk any more about it."

"When I went up for a commission," Henry said, "the Chairman of the Board just stared through me for a quarter of an hour while the rest asked questions. He was a big brute of a brigadier, with ginger whiskers. Then he looked at the notes in front of him and barked, 'Classics, eh?' I wasn't sure what he thought of Classics, but I had to say yes. He leaned forward and said, 'Brekekekex koax koax. Context?' I said '*The Frogs*, sir,' and that's how I became a British officer. It was the only Greek tag I knew. I realize now it was almost certainly the only one he knew, as well."

Tonight, Cynthia reflected, Henry was more animated than usual. His cheerfulness seemed inappropriate and, in an odd fashion, blameworthy—as though he could be expected to know of her betrayal and be saddened by it. Formulating it in that way, she was conscious of her own absurdity, and with that felt the old current of affection for him running once more. She put a hand on his arm, and he covered it with his own.

Peter and Heather were wandering on. Peter said, "Give me some credit—I did save the rest of the frogs. The bloke with the spade wanted to cut them all apart."

"And let them think you were sentimental?"

"No fear. I did it the Army way. Tore several stripes off them for not getting on with their hole. They were both on guard that night, and when I went to have a look the

71

following morning, every solitary frog was gone. Aren't you proud of me?"

Heather clutched his arm and swung on it. "You darling idiot! I adore you."

The pang of envy with which Cynthia saw them touch and kiss went deep. She eased her hand free of Henry's; he patted it as she did so, and then put his own hand back in his pocket. She envied him, too, for his contentment; and, for a moment only, she loathed Albrecht. He was a man—he could be content with the body's passion. She had been a fool to think she could. She knew now she loved Albrecht, utterly and hopelessly.

Heather turned around and called to Henry: "You haven't forgotten you're to show us your caves?"

"Yes, of course. Tomorrow afternoon?"

"Lovely! We'll be there."

"That great galumphing girl," Henry observed in comment. "But rather pleasant in her way, don't you think?"

THERE WAS thunder about when Albrecht drove them all back to the inn, and during the night Cynthia woke to hear rain dripping off the eaves. She could not understand, drowsed with sleep as she was, why it was so depressing that it should be raining, and drifted back out of consciousness with the thought still puzzling her mind.

In the morning she awoke completely fresh and with dismal comprehension: the rain would prevent her going riding with Albrecht. She humped the bedclothes over her shoulder with annoyance and stared at the white wall of the bedroom. She could hear Henry moving about. She asked him for a cigarette without looking around, and he brought it to her.

"Did you hear the storm in the night?"

She said wearily, "Yes."

"Unpleasant while it lasted."

She sat up in bed. The room was darker than was usual at this time of day, and the sky outside showed massive gray clouds; but it was not actually raining.

She said more hopefully, "Is it going to clear?"

"It's clearing already. The sun's shining at the far end of the valley."

She tried to warn herself that the capability of being moved so easily from depression to delight was one that could, in different circumstances, render her as vulnerable to pain, but she was in no mood for warning or analysis. It was enough that the sun would soon be shining.

She was uneasy during the early part of the morning; first in case the weather, precariously fine, with clouds resting on the greater part of the line of hills, should break again; and then over Heather's vacillation as to whether she would like to try another riding lesson. But the sun stayed out, and Heather decided in favor of another set of tennis; and they rode at last through the park, the hoofs of their horses scattering raindrops from the grass.

And now that the possible obstacles had proved nonexistent, she found herself in reaction—against the adventure, against Albrecht, against her own desire. She was thinking, as they rode, of the baldness and ugliness of it: that he would take her to the place they had gone to the previous day, and make love to her in the same way. She was to be used, with no profession of tenderness or love, by a man whose only true passion was for death. It was absurd and humiliating. However much she wanted to, she told herself, she would not submit to this. To do so was to betray not Henry, but herself.

Albrecht, however, did not lead her to the same spot, but to a point, farther up the valley, where the hill hid both *Schloss* and village from view. She wondered about this and then—her mind divided between amusement and further repulsion—found an explanation. There was a deep cleft in the face of the hill, overhung from above, and the fine sandy gravel which made up the floor of the cleft was dry and powdery. In all probability the rain never reached it.

She said, as Albrecht tethered the horses, "You could have brought a groundsheet, couldn't you? Or were you thinking of my reputation?"

He smiled but did not answer. They walked in silence up the last few yards of the slope, the walls of the cleft closing in on them, and loose stones scattering under their feet. When they sat down, their bodies did not touch. She felt herself prickling with anger—hoping for an approach so that she could reject it.

73

Albrecht nodded toward the other range of hills which faced them across the valley.

"It will rain again today. I know this kind of weather in these hills. The storms circle round and return."

She said with some petulance, "But we shan't get wet in this little nest, shall we?"

"No. We shall be dry here."

He reached out to take her hand, slowly and gently, as though caressing a child. She drew back from him.

He asked, "What is the matter, Cynthia?"

His tone almost disarmed her, but she was determined not to be disarmed.

She said, "Nothing. What should be the matter? We've managed to get away together, and you've found a nice dry spot for us out of the rain. Is there anything more to want?"

"I would like you to be happy."

"Of course. It's more pleasant that way, isn't it?"

After a moment he said, "If you would prefer it that we ride back . . ."

She gritted her teeth. "You're very obliging, Albrecht, aren't you?"

He did not attempt to touch her again, but his eyes sought her face, examining its expression with patient attention.

"Tell me why you are unhappy."

She asked incredulously, "Can you really see no reason why I should be?"

"No good reason."

"Do you think this is how it ought to be—planning and taking precautions, maneuvering and lying and deceiving? Do you really not mind the furtiveness of it?"

She thought she knew what he was thinking when he did not answer immediately: that on his side there had been no more than mild flirtation, that it was she who had been swept away by passion. That he would not make such a charge did not make the realization any less humiliating for her. She had brought it about and now, unreasonably, was complaining.

Albrecht said slowly, "If those two—Peter and Heather —were taken and put into a prison, where it was necessary for them to deceive their guards and lie to them so that they might be with one another for a time . . . would that distress you, or distress them?"

"There's a difference. They feel they have a right to each other, because they're in love."

74

"And do you think that is better—to deceive oneself instead of deceiving others?"

Her voice choking a little, she said, "How do you think of me, Albrecht—as a woman shamelessly offering herself to you, whom you took because it was easier to take her than to refuse her?"

He shook his head. "I told you—you are not like that. No one could think you were."

"But I did thrust myself on you, didn't I? If I hadn't—if I had gone on behaving toward you as I did that first time you kissed me—what would you have done? Nothing. You aren't sufficiently interested in me, in anybody. If you're a hedonist, it's only for the pleasure that comes easily to hand. There isn't anything that's worth taking trouble to get, is there?"

"It is not that." His brow wrinkled more deeply as he tried to find expression. "I kissed you because it seemed right to do so. I have never known another woman with whom there was that rightness. But to seek you against your desire would have been foolish."

"It made no difference at all then that I was a married woman?"

"No. If one believes in God, then it is possible to believe that marriage is sacred. If not, then it is no more than a contract made by two people, for their convenience. Once it is no longer convenient for either one of them, it cannot be enforced."

"You mean, the marriage is broken? Do you think my marriage is broken?"

"No. It has changed for you; that is all."

"Changed!" she said bitterly. "Just a little change—so that I have to spend my time deceiving and lying to the person who is closest to me. No more than that?"

He asked her gently. "Do you find it so hard?"

"Do you think it's easy?"

"It depends on the person."

She seized his hand which rested beside her, and in her fury tore at it with her nails. "Damn you! Damn you! You've done all this, and now you laugh at me."

Albrecht made no attempt to take his hand away. After a time she began to cry, and her head fell against him. His free hand touched her hair, stroking and easing. Her lips pressed themselves against the flesh that her nails had been scoring, and her tears dried into shaking sobs.

He said, "You will be better."

Listening to the quiet unhesitant voice, nuzzling against

75

the flesh wet with her tears, she grew calm again. She lifted her head and turned away from him to make up her face.

"I was not laughing at you," Albrecht said.

She was still not looking at him. She said, "I know." Her words were distorted as she put on lipstick, and she finished her mouth before she spoke again. "What you said was true—that's why I hated it. I do find it easy—easier than I could ever have imagined I would." Now she turned back, and their eyes met. "I hate myself for doing it so well. And I hate you a little, for helping me."

He said, "And most of all you hate it that when we two are alone together, we must make love—that being together has for us no other meaning than that?"

"Yes, I hate it."

He smiled. "Then it is simple. Today, at least, we will not make love. We will sit and talk like old friends. I will tell you tales about my country, and you will tell me how beautiful it is."

"Can we?"

"Why not? All is in the will, and the imagination. Today we are companions, who talk only."

She said, "You're a strange person, Albrecht."

"You told me so once before, and I asked you why. Do you remember?"

"Yes. The more I know of you, the stranger you seem."

"What is strange now?"

"That you're both selfish and considerate at the same time. I don't think I've ever known anyone who was more considerate."

"Or more selfish?"

She paused. "Perhaps. To want to die is selfish."

"And strange also?"

"Yes—in someone who enjoys life as you do."

"Tell me—do you know the custom by which a man who is condemned to die is given for his last meal whatever food he wishes to have?"

"I've heard of it. I don't know whether it is true."

"It has been true in many countries, at many times. Do you think, if you were such a one, you would have appetite for that meal?"

She shook her head. "How could I? One would choke on the food."

"You think that because you cannot believe you are to die. I was in a cell once, with two men. They were S.S., and the Russians had condemned them to death. They

76

were to die early in the morning, and I saw them eat their last meal. It was of bread and thin soup only—the Communists do not have the custom of which we spoke. One of the men was resigned to death; the other believed, until they came to take them out to be hanged, that death could not happen to him.

"It was this second man who could not eat his bread—not even drink the soup. He gave his share to the man who knew that within an hour the breath would be squeezed out of his body. I saw him eat the food with as much contentment as I have seen at any banquet, although he knew that it went to nourish a corpse."

"I suppose some people are unimaginative."

"No. It is not that. The truth is that when a man knows —deeply knows—that he is going to die, death no longer has terrors for him. It is the hope of living on that gives the fear of death. When that is gone, there is no fear."

"That's how it is with you?"

"Yes."

"But no one has condemned you to death."

"There need not be a condemning. We live because we have a passion for life. It is the strongest of all passions, but it can be broken, or worn away by life itself. Many people die because they choose to die."

"Old people."

"Old or worn or broken. It makes no difference."

The clouds in the sky were more ragged, trailing lower over the slopes of the hills. The skyline across the valley was hazy; it was possible that it was raining over there.

"The passion for life—when it has been broken, can it be restored?"

"I do not think so."

"Why not?"

"Because living is an absurdity. While the passion is there, we do not notice it. Afterwards we can see more clearly."

"How do you know you are seeing more clearly?"

"As a man who has been blind knows. Everywhere men and women busy themselves with the things that are important to them. They satisfy their senses, they look for the affection they missed in the cradle, they make plans so that others may know their importance. And in the end, the senses will die and the affections wither, and when the statue stands among the ruins, no one will know who carved it, or whose glory it honored."

77

"That's nonsense. Even if life has no meaning, it's more sensible to enjoy it than to reject it."

His eyes on the valley of the Frohn, Albrecht quoted:

"Werd' ich zur Augenblicke sagen,
Verweile doch, du bist so schön—
Dann magst du mich in Fesseln schlagen,
Dann will ich gern zugrunde gehen . . ."

He turned toward Cynthia. "That comes when Faust makes his compact with Mephistopheles. He has been given everything—knowledge, power, wealth. He may keep all those things, and his soul, too, until such a time as he cries, 'Stay to the moment as it passes—Stay, let me keep this.' And with that cry, he must lose everything, and lose his soul."

"And he loses?"

"Of course. He is a man. He seeks permanence, or the illusion of permanence. Without that, knowledge, power, wealth are not worth having."

"Nor love, neither?"

"Nor love. Love is the spirit warming its cold hands before a fire. But in time the fire will die out."

"Will it?"

"It must. Unless there is God, and eternity, and all the other things, it must die out. What else?"

"Then I'll believe in God, and eternity, and everything else. They might be true."

"Yes." The affirmation was in a tone of flat disbelief.

She said, "But don't you even wish they were true?"

"No. To want that is to want to live. The first rests on the second."

She turned the rings around on her wedding ring finger. "Do you realize how humilating it is for me to hear you talk like this?"

"We are friends," he said gently, "but we are different people. We have to let each other go as we must. There is no happiness in anything else."

She said unhappily, "There is no happiness in anything anyway, is there? Isn't that what you've been telling me? Haven't you been destroying my illusions with what you think is your truth?"

"Then I have said it badly. I have no truth. To want to live is one thing—to cease wanting is another. Neither is true nor false. To you I should seem no more than a de-

78

feated man—defeated by life and so turning away from it. That is truth for you."

She stared at him. "I want more than that."

He did not reply at once. Then he said, "I am sorry. I think maybe I should not have talked as I have done. With anyone else, I would not. Heather is right not to like philosophy; it serves no purpose except to disturb people."

"I'm glad you talked to me like that. It makes me miserable, but I'm glad all the same."

She leaned her head against his shoulder. He put his hand up to steady her; it was the hand she had scratched, and she saw for the first time the angry weals that had been raised on it.

"Oh, my poor darling!"

She sat up and took his hand, caressing it with her own. The words had sprung naturally and without forethought, but she realized after she had said them that this was the first endearment that had been offered between them. More than anything else, the realization made her conscious of the depth of her feelings, and of their hopelessness.

She turned to kiss him, her despair reflected in the recklessness and fierceness of her kisses. He kissed her back and then, for a moment, held her away from him.

"Are you sure . . . ?"

"Darling," she whispered, "darling . . . other people have years. We only have hours."

There was a sharp shower of rain late in the morning, and another while the four of them were having lunch together at the *Schloss*. These did not clear the air, however. Sunshine came in bursts from behind towering clouds that varied between blackness and a dazzling white, and there was a more or less constant rumble of thunder in the surrounding hills.

Heather said, as they went out to the Mercedes, "Lightning! Did you see it?"

"Not at all uncommon," Peter said, "when there's thunder about. I must say I like that sweater."

Heather, like Cynthia, was dressed in a sweater-and-slacks outfit, in roughly the same fashion as the two men. She had borrowed Cynthia's spare sweater, not having expected to need such equipment on an August honeymoon, and while a fit, it was undeniably a tight one.

"Lecher!" she told him. She whispered, "Sweetie, I feel naked in it."

79

Peter examined her critically before whispering back, "You don't look as good as that naked."

Albrecht reversed the car on the terrace, and headed for the Graz road. Cynthia was seated beside him in front, with Heather and Peter in the back seat.

Heather leaned toward Peter and muttered, "Right! People shouldn't have what they can't appreciate. From now on you'll see no more of me than Albert saw of Queen Victoria."

He grinned. "I was only joking."

"I wasn't," she whispered implacably.

He pulled her down against him. "Anyway, that doesn't mean anything. We don't know what V. and A. got up to."

As they rounded the slope of the Frohnberg, it was possible to see that the clouds were thicker and more menacing toward Graz.

Heather sat up abruptly. "Not a bad idea being under cover on a day like this."

Albrecht pulled the car over onto the verge. "A mountain is a leaky umbrella," he told her. "If there is rain, it may drip through."

"We'll be out by that time, won't we?"

"Yes. It takes some hours generally to filter through the earth. Peter, will you get the boots out of the back of the car?"

Henry waved to them from the other side of the road. They went across to join him, carrying the rubber wading boots. Cynthia had her own, and Albrecht had been able to find a pair for Peter as well as himself. He had discussed the possibility of getting a pair from Graz for Heather, but she had explained that she would prefer to have Peter carry her through any streams that required fording. She was wearing flat shoes.

Albrecht said to Henry, "You have come to meet us?"

"I thought I might as well, and have a breath of fresh air."

"I could have brought you back to have luncheon with us. It would have been more sensible."

"I'm used to snacks at midday," Henry said. "It gives me a better appetite for dinner. The weather outlook doesn't look awfully good, does it?"

"There will be a heavy storm yet. But I was telling Heather that it is not likely to affect us. There may be wetness from the rain last night, though."

"Yes. A nice steady drip in the stalactite cave."

80

"Building up the stalactites?" Peter suggested.

"Quite a lot." Henry smiled. "Probably at least a thousand millionth of an inch."

Peter tugged on a rubber boot. "Perhaps we ought to come back in a couple of hundred years and see the difference. Albrecht, I didn't think I had bigger feet than you."

"Fancy!" Heather said. "You delicate beauty."

"It is the boots," Albrecht said. "They are made to fit very tightly. Are we all ready to go in?"

"I'll climb on your back, shall I?" Heather asked Peter.

"Not until it's time. I can do a bit of snatch lifting, but I haven't got the stamina for long hauls. And certainly not for hauling you along that ledge and then plunging into the river with you."

They were under the cave mouth. Henry said, "The usual warning: no shouting—don't talk any more loudly than is necessary."

"Or else the roof falls in," Heather said.

Henry fitted on his helmet. "I'm the one who gets off lightest if it does," he said. "That beret won't protect you very much."

She said gloomily, "I don't think it will even protect what's left of my wave."

Henry switched on the light attached to the front of his helmet, and its beam fanned out to show the swift black waters of the Frohn and the walls, glistening with dampness, of the tunnel that enclosed it.

"I'd better go first," he said, "and Albrecht can bring up the rear with the other torch."

Cynthia allowed Heather and Peter to go in front of her, following Henry. She touched Albrecht's hand as they moved ahead into the darkness. They saw first Henry and then Peter slip over the ledge into the river, and afterwards there was the muted giggling disturbance as Heather was taken in Peter's arms.

Albrecht said, "It will be easier if I carry you also. The river is running deep here."

"Yes, please."

She bent her head down as he carried her, and pressed her lips against his neck. The others were splashing along in front of them.

"Do we need to go and see caves?"

"Not if you do not wish it." His voice, altogether quieter even than usual, still had an echo. "But then we must explain to the others."

81

For a moment she burrowed deeper with her face. She said at last, "It wouldn't be wise, would it? Never mind."

They climbed through into the first cave, where the others were waiting, and set off up the slope. Rubble scattered underfoot. The noise of the underground Frohn died away behind them and was replaced, as they came into the stalactite cave, by the sound of dripping water.

Heather squealed suddenly. The beams from the two torches converged to cover her.

Peter said, "What's the matter?"

"Water," Heather said indignantly. "It dripped down the back of my neck."

Henry said, "It will be worse further on, you know."

"It was the shock," she explained.

"You shouldn't let it provoke you into anything sudden —movements or cries." He added more sternly, "Otherwise we shall have to abandon the whole thing."

His light was still on her since he was facing in her direction. She stood there, blinking.

"I'll be good the rest of the way. I promise."

The beam of light swung away from Heather, traversing the fence of stalactites as Henry directed his attention toward the wooden ladder and the chimney. He mounted the steps, while Albrecht trained the other torch on him, and pulled himself forward. They saw him wriggle out of sight.

"You next," Peter said. "And don't scream if you see a mouse coming the other way."

Heather stared in horror. "Oh, heavens! I suppose I might." She looked up at the hole in the curving wall of the cave. "I don't think I dare."

"Since you haven't got a headlamp like Henry, you won't see it," Peter pointed out. "Get a move on, old girl."

"Not see it!" Heather exclaimed. "That's worse still."

Albrecht said, "He is joking, Heather. There are no mice in the caves."

"Are you sure?"

"Quite sure. Mice do not burrow far from the surface. You will find no mice here."

Henry's voice echoed down to them. "What's the hold-up?"

Heather mounted the ladder, with Peter close behind her. Albrecht held the light on them until they had gone. He said to Cynthia, "Now it is our turn."

"Give them time to wriggle through." She reached up and kissed him. "I am shameless, you know. Don't worry.

82

I rubbed my lipstick off as soon as we got inside the cave."

He said, "I am glad you are shameless."

With his arms around her, the light from the torch stabbed high over their heads toward the pointed arch of the ceiling. She shivered.

"Doesn't even this make you afraid of death?" she asked. "The darkness under the earth?"

He said softly, "We must go, Cynthia." He always had a little difficulty with the *th*. "Let me help you."

In the painted cave, they could hear the river's roar again. Henry collected them around him.

"The rest of the way is strange territory for all of you. I'll try to explain it in advance. You see how this cave slopes down toward the noise of the river? There's a crevice at the bottom which we have to get through."

Peter asked, "Big enough for Heather?"

There was a loudly whispered exclamation. "Brute!"

"That part's easy," Henry said. "It's about four feet wide, and there's a drop of about six feet. It's easily enough scaled on the way back. You drop onto another ledge running beside the Frohn. The tricky part is from there on. In places the ledge is very narrow—it will be necessary to feel your way along with your back against the wall. In other places, the rock comes down very low, and you'll have to crawl it. Fortunately the two don't coincide anywhere, or there would be nothing for it but to go into the river."

"Might it not be easier to do that since we have boots?" Albrecht asked him.

"I took the precaution of sounding the river. It's deep there—around waist-high most of the way along."

"Certainly no river in that case," Peter said with feeling. "I haven't forgotten my last encounter."

"Finally," Henry said, "there's the fact of the wall's being shaky. I'll warn you when we get to the particularly bad spots. But I'd like to repeat the general warning: no unnecessary noise, and all movements as gentle as possible. You all understand?"

Heather said indignantly, "Henry!"

"The warning is meant for everyone."

"But you looked at me, and your look's got a great big dazzling searchlight a couple of inches above it."

They saw him smile in the light from Albrecht's torch.

"Anyway, as long as it's understood, it doesn't matter. Now we can get on with it."

"Aren't we going to be roped together?" Heather asked.

83

"No, it's not necessary."

They set off down the slope, and Cynthia felt Albrecht's arm supporting her. The noise of the underground water grew steadily louder, its concentration increased by the fact that the roof of the cave sloped sharply down toward them as they descended. At the bottom there was the crevice Henry had described. It began as a crack in the rock floor, but widened rapidly. Henry sat on the edge, a couple of yards along, his feet dangling in darkness.

He bent his head so that his headlight showed them what lay below. The drop went at about forty-five degrees down to a rubble-strewn ledge several feet wide. Beyond the ledge there was the Frohn, rushing toward them out of the darkness beyond the lamp's ray, and disappearing again under the rock on which they stood.

Henry said quietly, "Here we are. Follow me down. I'll go ahead slowly. I'm making the beam as diffuse as possible so that it will be easy to follow; and as far as possible I'll try to throw the light down around my feet. Albrecht can shine along the ledge from behind."

There was no comment from either Peter or Heather; they scrambled down after Henry and made their way along the ledge. Albrecht went next, and looked up to Cynthia.

He said, "Come, my dear."

She felt a shiver of fear as she dropped. Her nerves were jarred by the continuous roar of water. As she reached the ledge, a stone rolled under her foot, and she began to fall forward. Albrecht took her and supported her.

Her slip had precipitated a general movement in the loose rubble; there was the noise of small rocks sliding, and a scatter of plops and splashes as they finished up in the river.

They found themselves lit up as Henry turned around to look in their direction.

He called, in a low urgent voice, "What's the matter?"

Albrecht replied, "Cynthia slipped. She is all right."

"We *must* go carefully," Henry said. "Any slip could be serious. Put your feet down as warily as possible. There are loose stones all the way along."

Darkness came around them again as he turned away.

Cynthia whispered savagely, "Does he think I slipped on purpose?"

"You are all right, are you not?" Albrecht asked her. "You did not hurt your ankle?"

84

"Kiss me," she told him. "Then I will be all right. Kiss me better."

They embraced briefly before setting out along the ledge. At intervals, instructions came from Henry:

"This is where the ledge narrows. Press your backs against the wall. . . . The wall's shaky for the next ten or fifteen yards. . . . You'll find the roof beginning to crowd down on you. You can manage it by stooping for a few yards yet, but then you will have to crawl. Keep your right side firmly against the wall."

She walked just in front of Albrecht, and the light from his torch was mainly thrown on the tumbling Frohn beside the ledge. She heard subdued murmurs from Heather and Peter, but it was a surprise when she emerged, quite unexpectedly, into the diffuse light of Henry's headlamp. He was standing, with Heather and Peter beside him, in the center of a cave and directing the light onto the opening of the tunnel into which the river poured.

The cave was shaped something like a squat bottle. It was only about half the size of the stalactite cave and, apart from the flat end where it was traversed by the river, was roughly circular. The bottle effect was provided by the surrounding walls, which ran vertically upward for about twenty feet before bending inward to form a neck. The top was lost in shadow.

Albrecht emerged and used his torch to provide an additional light on the cave. He flashed it directly upward, but the shadows remained defiant.

Henry said, "Here we are."

"Is this all?" Heather asked.

For reply, Henry directed his light over the top of the tunnel. Suddenly color flashed from a thousand reflecting surfaces, a million needle points—milky white, red, harsh green and black. The whole of the wall was in sharp-edged petrified blossom.

Heather gasped in wonder. "What are they?"

"Gypsum flowers."

"Can we pluck them?" Heather asked.

"I'll try and get a bit off for you before we go back. They look like flowers, don't they?" He shifted the light farther along. "Look at that rose bush!"

Albrecht said, "And this is the farthest point?"

"The farthest so far. There's a possible way that may go deeper." He turned his head, and the light swung around the cave. "I've brought a certain amount of gear in and I'd

85

like to have a try before I go back. Come over and I'll show you."

Heather said, "I'd rather look at the flowers."

"Leave me your torch," Peter said to Albrecht. "You can go by Henry's for the time being."

Cynthia went with Albrecht and Henry. They crossed to the point farthest from the river, where a heap of rubble lay against the wall. A store of equipment had been neatly laid out alongside it. Henry's light shone up the rubble pile towards the wall.

"See that?"

"Is it a hole?" Albrecht asked. "Surely, a very small one."

"About six inches, but I think it can be enlarged—the edges are friable. Anyway, I plan to have a go at it with a hammer."

"It does not look promising," Albrecht said doubtfully.

"I agree. But there's a current of air blowing through it. I find that . . ."

There was a sound from the other side of the cave, and Henry swung round quickly. His headlamp illumined Heather and Peter. Heather was holding Albrecht's torch; Peter was climbing the wall beside the tunnel mouth, his feet struggling for purchase against the rock.

Henry's voice was pitched low, but unmistakably urgent. "Get off that!"

"It's all right," Heather said. "He's just getting me that big red tulip."

"For God's sake, not that wall! Peter! Come down."

Peter's voice, muffled and echoing, said, "Righto."

They saw him feeling for a descent and, in the same instant, saw the wall crack and shatter above his head. Heather screamed, but her scream was buried in the ripening thunder of stone breaking and crashing against stone. The wall burst inward, as though a meteoric fist had smashed it. It took several seconds for the noise to die away, and for them to realize that Heather was still screaming.

7.

THEY FOUND Heather lifting Peter up. He had not been buried by the rock, but had been thrown down near the edge of the water. She looked up incredulously into the light.

"He's all right!"

Peter himself said, "I guess I pulled the wrong string. Quite a surprise packet. I'm afraid I didn't get you your flower, honeybunch."

She leaned over him, recovered from her first relief. "Are you sure there's nothing broken?"

"Only my nerve."

Henry said, "I'm glad you're all right, Peter." His voice was coldly incisive. "But that was a damn stupid thing to do."

"You didn't tell him not to," Heather protested.

"I hardly thought I needed. I told you all several times that the tunnel wall was unsafe. If it was risky to speak above a whisper, what do you think the weight of a six-footer was likely to do?"

Peter said, "You're quite right. I ought to have known better."

"Anyway," Heather said, "nothing serious has happened. Everything's all right."

"Is it?"

The light from the headlamp covered the place where the mouth of the tunnel had been. There was none there now. The collapsed wall lay in a heap of shattered rock against which the river waters broke in angry black foam. Here and there a patch of gypsum blossom winked up in the light.

They all stared for a moment in silence.

Albrecht said, "You have not shovels here among your equipment, Henry?"

"It wouldn't do much good if I had. We should want a couple of bulldozers to cope with that. And there's the river to consider."

Peter said grimly, "I've torn it properly, haven't I?"

87

"How long shall we have to wait," Heather asked, "to be rescued? I've got some chocolate with me."

Henry said slowly, "No one is going to rescue us along that route."

"Why not? They'll know something's happened when we don't get back for tea. They will have spades and everything. If you get enough people digging away at it, I don't see why you couldn't clear it."

None of the others spoke.

Heather said impatiently, "Well, why not? Even if we have to spend a couple of days in here, we can manage. We shan't die of thirst."

"No," Henry said, "we shan't do that."

His light shone on the broken stone and the water swirling against it.

Albrecht asked quietly, "How long?"

"It's impossible to say—but you can count it in hours, and not many, either."

"How long till *what*?" Heather asked.

Peter said, in a dry voice, "The river's blocked by the fall. You can see that the level's rising already. It will spread out over the floor of this cave. Gradually it will fill it. That's what they're talking about, darling."

She stared in awakening horror at the water.

"You mean—we'll drown?"

Peter said desperately, "If we really had a go at the tunnel—even if we didn't clear a way. through for ourselves, we might make a channel for the river."

"I suppose it's possible," Henry said, "but without any proper tools, I don't think our chances would be very good. We would waste time and exhaust ourselves to no purpose."

Heather said, "Is it better to sit still and wait till the water comes up and drowns us?"

Henry said, almost absently, "There's really only one thing we can do, isn't there?"

Heather began, "I'm not going to . . ."

Albrecht said, "Your hole? But that means going farther into the earth, does it not? If we cannot find a way out from here, how can we do so from more deeply inside the hill?"

"The current of air," Henry said, "means that somewhere there is another link-up with the outside world. God knows how far or inaccessible, but it offers a chance. It might lead us to the Liedl caves."

"But Liedl is many kilometers from Frohnberg."

88

"By road. Not so far if you go through the hill."

Peter said, his voice barely hopeful, "So we could follow the air current until it brought us out somewhere—perhaps to Liedl?"

"I don't think we have any other chance," Henry said. "If we stay here, we're finished."

"Well," Heather said, "what are we waiting for? If it's the only thing to do, we might as well do it."

Henry said sharply, "One thing we're waiting for is to find that torch you dropped." He swung his head from side to side, scanning the cave floor with the light. "One match may make the difference between getting out or being trapped."

Heather said, "It *might* be under that loose rock."

"You two can hunt for it," Henry said. "I've got a spare torch over the other side that you can use. But from now on, we're practicing absolute economy. Turn your pockets out for anything that might be useful."

They all responded to the command in his voice. Cynthia, rummaging in the pockets of her slacks, reflected that this was a Henry she had never known before; except, by unconfirmed inference, in the photograph of the severe young captain that had stood by her bedside during the war's latter years.

She said, "Handkerchief and compact. Nothing else."

Albrecht produced a silver cigarette case. "With thirteen cigarettes. A lighter. And some money. I suppose the money is useless."

"Packet of ten," Peter said. "And a box of Swan Vestas."

"Good," Henry said. "Heather?"

"I don't need to look," she said cheerfully. "I know I haven't got anything."

"Are you sure?"

"Do you want to search me? I have a husband to give me cigarettes and light them."

"What about the chocolate you said you had with you?"

"Oh, that." She produced the packet. "I thought you were talking about lights and things."

Henry took the packet from her. "Look," he said, "I want to have everything straight. Even if we can get out of this cave, it isn't going to be easy to find a way that will get us through to the open. It wouldn't be easy if we were all experienced cavers. As it is, our only hope is that you all do exactly as I tell you—no arguments, no evasions. Is that perfectly clear?"

They nodded. Heather said, "Sorry, Henry."

"Never mind. I'll get you the other torch, and you can look for the one you lost. Albrecht, you can lend me a hand on widening the hole."

They all trailed after him to the other side of the cave, and then Heather and Peter, having been given a torch, went back. The other three remained.

Henry said, "We might as well take an inventory."

"There seems a lot of stuff here," Cynthia said. "Lucky for us you brought it all along."

"There isn't a tenth of what I would like," Henry said gloomily. "Let's have a look. Light, first. How's the battery in that torch of yours, Albrecht—providing they find it?"

"It is quite new. I am not sure how long they last."

"Say three hours. I've got spare betteries, but they will only fit my headlamp and the other torch. Headlamp—about two hours, with three four-hour refills. Spare torch —quite unused, and another three refills: fifteen or sixteen hours altogether. Two spare bulbs. Then there's the acetylene lamp—" he nodded his head toward it—"two and a half hours—and enough carbide to recharge half a dozen times, making about seventeen hours. That's a total of just over forty-eight hours of light."

"We shan't need all that, shall we?" Cynthia asked.

"In addition, *Gott sei Dank*, half a dozen candles, and two boxes of matches in watertight containers, apart from Albrecht's lighter and Peter's box of Swan Vestas."

"But almost no food," Albrecht said.

"I wouldn't trade a solitary match for a loaf of bread," Henry said. "It's light that we've got to have. We can live on our fat for longer than the time it would take for the last glimmer of the last match to die away. But if we find ourselves wandering in the dark, we're finished."

"Wandering," Albrecht said. "It may be that there is nothing on the other side of the wall—nothing that can offer us a way."

"Then we're finished anyway. Food, now. One small tin of dry biscuits. Two tins of meat. Three small packets of mixed nuts and raisins. Four bars of dried banana. Two half-pound bars of milk chocolate and one—" he fished Heather's packet out of his pocket—"quarter-pound bar of chocolate praline."

Albrecht said, "No. They are two-hundred- and hundred-gram bars. Five hundred grams altogether. That is not much more than an English pound."

"Yes, of course. One container for a quart of water."

90

"Water!" Cynthia said. "We have too much of that."

"Here we do, but we've got a lot farther to go. I hope much of the way is going to be dry. I should like to be able to carry more than a quart."

"I do not think we will go far in these caves without encountering water," Albrecht said.

"I'm afraid you're right, but we'll hope not. Now, gear. Two hundred-foot lengths of half-inch nylon rope, two thirty-foot electron ladders, a dozen T-section pitons and a dozen angle irons, a chisel and a short hammer. And one—" he paused lovingly—"inflatable RAF-type rubber dinghy."

"That won't hold five of us," Cynthia observed.

"No. It will take two, though. If we have to use it, we'll have to do the kind of thing they do in those puzzles about missionaries ferrying cannibals across rivers."

"Do you think there might be lakes?"

"I think there might be one, at least, from the speed with which the level of the Frohn rises at times. That's what I brought the boat down for. I'm very glad I did. It improves our chances quite a lot."

Cynthia said, "I suppose it does."

"Here's the hammer and chisel," Henry said. "Will you get up there and start opening it out, Albrecht? I'll sort out the stuff here."

"I have no light," Albrecht pointed out.

"I'll shine your way up. Once you've found the hole, you can work in the dark for a bit. It's only a matter of chipping away."

They saw him climb up the rubble slope and settle himself into position. There was the clang of steel on stone, and Henry let his head drop again as he looked at the equipment in front of them.

"We've got to divide these up," Henry said. "Two lengths of rope, two ladders, and the boat. Something for everyone. You and Heather had better have the ladders, and I'll take the dinghy. If it gets holed, we're sunk, literally. I haven't got a repair outfit. I'll take eight of the irons and the hammer, as well, and we'll share the rest out. Albrecht can carry the rucksack with the food."

Cynthia said quietly, "Henry?"

"Yes."

"What chance have we?"

"Very good, provided we keep our heads."

"You shouldn't lie to me."

He lifted his head to look at her; the light from his

91

lamp dazzled her eyes. But even without that, it would not have been possible to see the expression on his face, which was in the shadow, lit only by the occasional stray beam from the torch on the other side of the cave.

Henry said slowly, "No, we shouldn't lie to each other."

"Well?"

"What I said about the current of air was quite true. Somehow that hole up there must lead to the outside world. We may find ourselves safe half an hour after getting through it."

He paused, and she waited.

"The only trouble is that a current of air can go where men and women can't—up a smooth vertical chimney, or over an underground river with the rock an inch or two from the water all the way. We just don't know what it's going to be like. We shan't know until we try it."

"If the first thing happened—" she said—"finding a way out quickly—that would be very lucky, wouldn't it?"

"Very lucky."

"And the second? Darling, you must tell me. You have some idea of what the chances are in caves like this."

"They're all different."

"Tell me."

He said heavily, "The second's more likely."

"Much more likely?"

"Yes."

Not speaking for a moment or two, she was deeply conscious of the other noises about them: the tap and scrape of Albrecht's chisel, the distant chatter of Heather and Peter, and the implacable rushing gurgling of the river.

She said, "If there hadn't been this hole in the wall here, it would have been over quicker, wouldn't it?" Henry did not answer her. "We may be saving ourselves for something worse."

He turned his head up to where Albrecht was crouched, spotlighted for the moment.

"I don't think there could be anything worse than being drowned here by slowly rising water. There is a chance of our getting out."

She wanted to touch him, to turn for comfort to his arms, but she could not bring herself to the gesture. "We shouldn't lie to each other." She had taken the risk that adultery might ruin the rest of her life with Henry; but she had not known that the life might be so short, nor that it could sit like a ghost between them even in the shadow of death. She still did not know what it was she felt for

92

Albrecht, but it was something capable of turning her heart to the same dry coldness that possessed his. She tried desperately to love Henry as she had always loved him, spurring herself on with the fear of death, but it was no good.

Heather's voice echoed through the cave. "Got it!" There was a whispered protest from Peter, and then the two of them advanced toward Henry, each carrying a torch.

Heather said happily, "Sorry about the shout. Look, it's quite all right—not even scratched." She flashed the torch up and around the cave.

Henry reached out and took it from her hand.

"Can't I keep it?" she asked. "You've got one."

"This is for Albrecht," Henry said. "Peter, you can keep the one you've got."

"Well, I don't see why the men should have torches and not the women."

Henry ignored her. He said to Peter, "We shan't use these at all—at least, to begin with. As long as we can use the acetylene lamp, we might as well. For one thing, it gives a wider light, and for another, if we run into a really wet pitch it will be useless. We might as well get the advantage from it while we can. What's the river level like?"

"It's up over the top."

"I expected that." He called up to Albrecht, "How are you getting on up there?"

"I have made it bigger, but now the stone breaks less easily."

"I'll come up and lend a hand with a couple of irons." To Cynthia he said, "Spread the equipment as I told you. Try to get a comfortable fit with it. You may have to carry it a long way, and over difficult ground."

He began to clamber up the slope towards Albrecht.

Heather said, "Can we have a light on down here?"

He turned back toward them, enveloping them with light. "Peter can use the torch, but as little as possible. You might as well learn to handle things in the dark."

"Damn it," Heather said. "It's all right for you—you've got a permanent searchlight in front of you."

"So I have." Cynthia knew all the intonations of his voice; now, for the first time since the rock fall, there was strain in it. "If someone else would like the job of trying to get us out of this, he can have the cap and headlamp. Or she."

He turned back toward Albrecht, and they heard the two of them murmuring together.

"Squashed," Heather said. "I suppose he's right. What a masterful husband you've got, Cyn. I really wanted a light to go away and spend a penny. And I don't dare ask him. Darling, will you be weak and let me borrow yours? I'll take the blame if Henry says anything."

Peter handed her the torch. "Mind you don't fall in the river. And use it as little as possible."

"Sweetums, I don't exactly want to have myself flood-lit."

Left in the dark with Peter, Cynthia found it easy and natural to do what she had not been able to do with Henry; she put her hand on his arm for comfort. He took it and squeezed it reassuringly.

She said, "Bless you for that."

"For what?"

She would have liked to tell him: for demonstrating that it was still possible for her to feel a man's hand upon her own without being conscious either of guilt or desire. For a moment he was dearer to her than either Henry or Albrecht.

He said gloomily, "What a mess I've landed us all in."

"It wasn't your fault."

"I'm always doing something like that. All my life I've had the credit for being capable and level-headed, and every now and then I've done something so damn silly that it's made people stand aghast. Like the time in the Army when I misread a simple map reference and threw a colossal scheme of maneuvers into utter confusion."

Overhead, the chipping steadily continued.

Cynthia said, "I shouldn't worry about it. Heather's very cheerful, isn't she?"

"She's wonderful," Peter said. "You all are. I'm the only one who's scared silly. I suppose we may get out easily enough, but all I can think of is the thousands of tons of rock over our heads."

He was looking to her for comfort—to the older woman, to whom his dignity as a male did not matter. It was her turn to squeeze his hand.

"We're all scared—except Heather, perhaps. And you're putting up as good a show of not showing it as anyone."

"If I hadn't been such a fool . . ."

"Never mind. Here's Heather."

94

Light wavered toward them from the other side of the cave.

"The river," Heather complained, "started lapping around my feet." She shone the torch backward, and they saw the black sheet of water, now more than halfway across the cave floor. "What's made it get such a rush on?"

"It's over the ledge," Peter said. "The rest of the cave is more or less flat."

"All right for you with your rubber boots, but I'm going to get my feet wet."

"You can have one of mine," Peter said, "and we'll each stand on one leg like storks." He called up to Henry, "How's it going there?"

Henry said, "You haven't got a spare stick of dynamite, I suppose?".

"Can't you chisel it? The water's coming up." His voice was urgent—too obviously so.

Henry called, "Don't worry. We're nearly through. But you can get the gear up on the slope above the water level. There's no point in getting it wet unnecessarily."

"I suppose," Heather said doubtfully, "it's really frightfully exciting—being trapped underground on one's honeymoon. Something to keep us going at parties for the next six months at least. But I wish we were already back there, talking about it. At Basil's place, for instance, with all those discreet lights and oodles of gin."

Peter, flashing the torch from time to time, was engaged in shifting the equipment up onto the rubble.

"Just imagine," he said, "that I should ever have come to think of the sight of Basil's face with pleasure."

"You can't have anything *against* Basil."

"Except that he tried to seduce you the week after we got engaged."

Heather giggled. "Yes. He told me that normally he only made love to married women, but you were such a reliable character that he would make an exception."

The chipping above them stopped. They heard Henry talking to Albrecht. "I think you're a little slimmer than I am. See if you can get through now. You might be able to clear it a bit more from the other side."

There was a scuffling noise.

Peter said, "My God, I hope he makes it."

"Are you through?" Henry asked. "What's it like?"

They could not make out Albrecht's answer. Henry said, "Right. You chip the bottom and I'll carry on at this side."

"What is it like?" Cynthia called up.

"There's a floor only a couple of feet down. So far, so good. It shouldn't be long before we can all get through, now." His voice held relief.

Heather said, "What is so good about that?"

"The hole's about twenty feet high in this cave—it could have been a hundred feet above the floor level in the next," Peter explained. "We should have had to go down on a rope. It wouldn't have been easy, and anyway we want to go up, not down."

The chipping stopped again after a few minutes. Henry slithered down the rubble slope, his headlamp glaring on them and on the spreading expanse of water behind them.

"All right," he said. "Generally, I'll go first, and Albrecht can take up the rear, but as he's already gone through we'll change over for this bit. You're Number Two, Peter, and Heather and Cynthia can follow you. Pick up your things. I'll carry Albrecht's for the present."

She would be with Albrecht, then, for whatever lay ahead of them. She did not know whether the thought was comforting or hateful. She had no real hope of their getting through safely. They would die; either quickly in some cataclysm or slowly of exhaustion. The prospect made more sharp the ambivalence of her own feelings. She wanted Albrecht as she had never, in all her life, wanted any other person; but she wanted Henry as well, with a wanting that, although less urgent and for the moment quite non-physical, was even more deeply-rooted.

She said to Henry, "You don't want me with you?" She had tried to make the question light; it came out flat and impersonal.

Henry said, "We need two men in front for tackling obstacles, and the third at the rear to help you and Heather. I think Albrecht is the best man for that."

"Keep the fool in the middle," Peter said, "where he can do the least damage."

"It's not a question of that. There's no limit to the damage any one of us can do, whatever position we are in."

"Are we going to be roped?" Cynthia asked.

"Not unless we have to be. It cuts down mobility for people who aren't used to a lifeline. Come on, then. Everything loaded? You and Heather first, Peter."

While they were scrambling up toward the hole, Henry turned his headlamp, for the last time, on the cave which they were abandoning. The water level was very close to where they stood. Its steady, almost perceptible rising was frightening. Cynthia thought of what it would be like in a few hours, with the cave flooded to more than three times a man's height, and the water still steadily pouring in, and out again through the hole in the wall.

She said, "It will follow us, won't it? The water."

"It may not. We don't know what the ground's like on the other side. In any case, I hope we can get well above this level."

She said softly, "I've been thinking—there's one good thing."

"What?"

"We none of us have children to leave."

He took hold of her wrists; his touch was the touch of a stranger—harsh, meaningless.

He said, "You mustn't talk like that, Sinner."

"How would you like me to talk—like Heather, as though this were some sort of undergraduate lark?"

"Yes, if that's the only alternative. It's going to be hard, desperately hard. The only chance we have is to refuse to admit, even to ourselves, just how desperate it is."

"Isn't that a bit silly?"

"No. Concentrate on remembering that life is worth living. Even without children, we've got something to fight for. Haven't we?"

"Yes, I suppose we have."

He lifted his head to where Peter's figure was wriggling through the hole.

"You go first. Can you manage that ladder?"

"Yes, easily."

The hole was quite small, but the rock wall which it pierced was not thick. Albrecht helped her down. There was a sudden glow from the cave they had left, and then Henry passed the acetylene lamp through. Its softer, more diffuse light lit up the place in which they now were. Albrecht took the lamp, and they all looked about them.

They stood in a gallery, about ten feet high, and four or five feet wide. The walls had been scoured by water, and the floor was runneled and broken. There was an upward slope, not steep but unmistakable, from left to right.

"Reassuring," Peter commented.

"Except for my poor feet on that floor," Heather said. "Come on, Henry; let's get you through."

Henry joined them. He gave the coil of rope to Albrecht, and in his turn studied the lie.

"It could be a lot worse," he observed. "At any rate, we

don't have to worry about what happens when the water starts coming through that window."

"We're traveling up, I take it," Peter said.

"Wherever we can. It may not always be possible. But this is a good start, and the current of air is from above. Is everyone sorted out? We want to try to keep on the move as long as we are using light."

Heather said, "We couldn't have a little snack first? I'm truly truly ravenous."

"We will eat at the beginning and end of the day," Henry told her.

"Can't we call it the end of the day? It's black enough, surely."

Henry looked at his watch. "It's four o'clock. We shall call it a day at nine, providing we can find a reasonable place to sleep."

"Sleep!" Heather echoed. "Down here? On bare rock?"

"I think you will be tired enough by that time to sleep anywhere. Especially after feasting on a coupld of squares of chocolate. I'm dividing the rations to last three days."

"Three days!"

Henry looked at her. "After that, we'll have to tighten our belts."

"But we aren't going to be three days down here," Heather protested. "The idea's silly."

"I hope you're right. But I'm not taking any chances. If we make it sooner, we'll have an orgy."

"I've always liked orgies," Heather said, "but I've never liked saving up for them. Well, I suppose it saves me slimming later on."

"Let's get moving, then," Henry said.

About thirty yards on, the gallery deviated to the left, narrowed to some extent, and began to dip instead of rise.

Cynthia heard Peter say, "Do you think we ought to turn back and try the other way? This is going down now."

Henry's voice came back hollowly, "Once you decide on a route, it's best to follow it through until it proves to be quite impossible. It can be fatal to start backtracking because you think you ought to have taken a different turning. The whole picture may change at any minute."

"The sooner this changes," Heather said, "the better. I don't like tight squeezes."

"Take another reef in your brassiere," Peter told her. "You'll manage."

98

Their progress became slower, not only owing to the narrowing of the gallery, but by reason of the increasingly broken nature of the floor. Heather, at one point, stumbled and fell. While Peter was helping her up, Cynthia put her hands out to touch the enclosing rock; it was only a matter of inches from her shoulders on either side.

Albrecht stood close behind her. She leaned backward, and he put his hands under her elbows, supporting her. No words passed between them. She shivered.

He asked her, "Are you cold?"

She whispered, "No. Just an awful feeling."

"What about?"

"Silly, I suppose. That all this might be a punishment. For . . ." She did not finish.

Albrecht said quietly, "And Henry, too—and Heather and Peter?"

"Yes, it's silly. But I was just realizing that—even if it were—I couldn't be sorry. Not really sorry."

His hands lightly touched the outlines of her breasts.

"Why should you be?"

Soon her shoulders were brushing against the walls; the others must already be having to squeeze their way through. The ceiling had dropped as well. Projections of rock caught at her hair. The light from the acetylene lamp, largely cut off by Henry's body, was no more than a variable glow toward which they stumbled.

Heather said, "This is no good." Her voice had begun to sound dispirited. "Can't we go back?"

For a few moments there was no reply. Then Henry called back, "It's all right. We're through."

They squeezed their way along the last few yards. The gallery opened out quite unexpectedly into another chamber. It was low-roofed, but very wide; the light did not reach to the far side.

"We're still underground," Heather said disappointedly. "I thought you meant through to the outside."

"We're out of that damned tunnel, at least," Peter said. "That's something."

"This cave—" Cynthia asked—"it's deeper underground than the one we were in before, isn't it? That passage went down for longer than it went up, and more steeply."

Henry peered out into the darkness. "This is the biggest room we've found in these caves so far. It may mean this is a pretty extensive system, and the more extensive the system the better."

"Why is that?" Albrecht asked.

"It makes it more likely that it joins up with the caves at Liedl. Anyway, the thing to do now is explore it. Our best plan is to track around the sides, making a note of all the openings and galleries leading off. I'll go to the right, and Albrecht can go to the left. The rest of you can have a rest here. Albrecht, flash your torch across to where you imagine I will be every five minutes. Stay there until you get an answering flash. If you don't get one, make your way back. Is that clear?"

Albrecht nodded. "Yes, it is clear."

"Put out the acetylene lamp," Henry ordered. "It will cost us a match to relight it, but that's less expensive than using up the carbide."

The two women sat on either side of Peter, their backs against the wall of the cave. Darkness had closed over them again; there was only the distant flicker of the torches as the two men made their way in opposite directions round the cave. From small movements, whispers, Cynthia could tell that Heather was caressing Peter. Feeling herself an intruder, she drew a little away from him, but he pulled her back.

"I hope you don't mind, Cynthia. I want company—the more the better."

She allowed herself to be brought against the hollow of his shoulder. Speaking across him to Heather, she said, "You've got a very nice husband, you know."

Heather said, "Mm-mm. Adorable. The nicest one I ever will have."

"You're embarrassing me," Peter said.

"But watch that little shy boy stunt," Heather warned. "It doesn't mean he's not dangerous."

AS THE TWO MEN approached, Peter said, "Do we move now?"

Henry said, "Yes. Pass the acetylene lamp, and I'll light it again."

"You're back more quickly than I expected," Peter said. "I thought you would want to recce the tunnels to some extent before deciding on one."

The match flared, and the lamp gave out its brilliance, making them blink.

"It was easier than we thought," Henry said. His face was grimly ironic. "There aren't any tunnels. Apart from the one we've just left."

"My God!" Heather exclaimed. "We aren't going back along that passage, are we?"

Cynthia thought of the dammed river in the chamber they had left, of the water steadily rising toward the escape hole and then pouring as steadily down the corridor into the mountain's unknown deeps. Fear death by drowning . . . and in a narrow drain, hundreds of feet underground.

She said, "If you don't mind, I'll stay. I'd rather die a dry death."

Henry said without expression, "You're going to do as I tell you, Sinner. If I decide we have to go back down there, then you're coming with us. It wouldn't be very nice, but there may be things even less pleasant before we find our way out of here. All the same, I hope it won't be necessary. There aren't any tunnels, but on the side I covered there's a sloping crack in the wall. I think it's been a water course at some time. I couldn't do much because I didn't have the irons with me."

"Might we be able to climb it?" Peter asked.

"We're going to try. But let's get moving right away, in case we have to go back down again."

The crack began two or three feet up from the floor, and ran away at an angle of about forty-five degrees, becoming wider and deeper until it was lost in the shadows. The edges of the crack were not sharp but worn smooth, possibly by the action of water.

Albrecht said, "If it were at one time a waterfall, would not the cave floor here be worn also?"

Henry was preparing to hammer in the first iron.

"Not if this were a shallow lake then." He hammered the piton into the rock face with steady powerful blows of the hammer while Albrecht held the lamp; the noise echoed and re-echoed in the great ringing bowl of the cave. "I think that one will do. Pass me another iron, Peter."

Gradually he began to ascend the slope. He tucked several irons in his belt and they could see him, fifteen or twenty feet above their heads, resting on the irons which had already been driven in, and hammering others in above them. He switched on his helmet light and its beam

101

showed them the cave roof; it was perhaps six feet above him.

In a flat voice, Peter said, "He must have been wrong about it being a water course."

"But the edges are worn," Albrecht insisted.

"There was probably water in here, but it came up from below, up that passage. Unless there's a hole somewhere in the roof. But we couldn't find it, or reach it if we found it."

Heather said, "You mean we'll have to go down again, after all? Oh, darling, please, no!"

"He still climbs," Albrecht said.

They watched Henry drive in yet another iron ahead of him. He moved up and rested against it. The light moved in a slow arc as he turned his head to examine the rock face above him. Then, slowly and carefully, he began to make his way back down toward them.

Heather gave a small moan of distress and put her head against Peter's chest. Henry continued to descend.

Albrecht called, "Will you not pull out the irons? May it not be that we will need them for other climbs?"

Henry said, "I still need them for this one." He dropped off the last iron to stand beside them. "Can I have one of the ladders?"

Peter asked incredulously, "You mean there's a way up there? But we could see the roof just above you."

Henry looked up the slope, the light from his headlamp glinting off the slanting row of irons.

"It looks dead from here, but there's a lip just above the last iron. You can't see it until you're almost abreast of it. Once I've got a ladder anchored up there you'll find it's easy enough."

"What's up there?" Cynthia asked. "Another hole to crawl through?"

"Better than that." He smiled, and the momentary relaxation of his features made her conscious of the tenseness that they had shown before. "Wait and see."

"A way out!" Heather exclaimed.

Henry shook his head. "Not yet." He tied the coil of ladder on his back. "I don't think we need bother with a lifeline; there's enough overhang to make the ladder lie clear of the face." He untied one of the ropes and took the free end. "I'll knot this onto the irons on the way up and pull them out behind me."

They had nothing to do but watch his slow painstaking climb. With the rope knotted on the two irons next in line,

102

he reached down to the one behind him and with a sharp tug snaked it free. The procedure was repeated again and again as he mounted the rock face.

Peter said, "It's wrong that Henry should have all the hard graft."

"He is the only one of us," Albrecht said, "who has experience in these things. There is no choice. Without him we are lost."

"We're just as lost if he gets exhausted. He could have had a rest and let you and me recce the cave."

Albrecht nodded his head at the cleft up which Henry was climbing. "Would you have seen this as a possible way?"

Peter did not reply. There was a cry from above them. "Ladder coming!" The frail-looking contraption clattered down the rock face toward them. The top of the ladder was lost in the overarching blackness.

Heather said, "Surely that thing won't bear our weight! I'd rather have climbed up the irons."

"It's misleading," Peter said. "It would take a woman twice your size. All the same, I think this might as well be a case of gentlemen first." He swung himself cautiously onto the ladder. "You can bring up the rear, Albrecht, in case they want a leg up."

Cynthia watched Peter's steady climb, followed by that of a much less steady and more voluble Heather. She understood the reason both for the unsteadiness and the volubility when it was her turn to go. The ladder seemed no less frail when she was actually on it; it swayed from side to side with the slightest movement she made, and her toes and knuckles were banged against the rock face. The rubber boots she was wearing protected her feet to some extent, but made the business of climbing more difficult. The last few rungs would have been impossible if it were not for Peter's hand stretched down to help her.

Henry had belayed the top of the ladder on a couple of irons driven into the ground, and was watching them to make sure they held firm. The only light was from his headlamp, which lit up a small area that included the lip of rock over which they had climbed.

Henry said, "Tell Albrecht to hold on down there. I'm going down myself and we'll see about getting the rest of the gear up. Watch these irons, Peter. I think they're O.K., but it's best to be sure."

As Henry disappeared down the ladder, Heather said, "I

wonder what it's like up here. Flash your torch, darling. Let's have a look around."

"I'm not sure we ought," Peter said. "Still, perhaps just a little flash . . ."

He directed the beam of the torch from the top of the ladder into the surrounding blackness. They had a glimpse of a vaulting chamber, stretching away all around them, of great gleaming pillars and a flash of crystal fire. Then Peter swung the torch back to light up the projecting irons which held the ladder.

Heather gasped. "But it can't be! We've climbed through a crack in the roof of that other cave. We can't possibly be in another one ten times as big."

"The whole damned mountain must be hollow," Peter said. "I can see now what old Henry was grinning about. This looks a bit better than squeezing back down that rat hole."

The cheerful exultancy of his tone provoked Cynthia into replying, "Does it matter how big a grave is?"

Peter said, "You must admit this makes things look better. We're getting somewhere, at any rate."

There were so many answers to that, Cynthia thought; but none of them were worth making, any more than her original remark had been. If they wanted to fool themselves with optimism, it did no good to dispute it. It was probably the kind of self-deception that was a natural part of having something—some hope or some illusion—to live for. She smiled unhappily to herself in the dark: she had something in common with Albrecht, at last.

When everything was up at the new level and the ladder and rope had been re-coiled, Henry lit the acetylene lamp again and they were able to see their surroundings more clearly. They had come up, as was now plain, through a jagged hole at the base of one wall of the higher chamber. Unlike the previous cave, this one was very high. Here, at its end, it was only about twenty feet across, but it seemed to stretch away for a great distance.

The walls were considerably encrusted with stalactite formations, ranging from shining narrow spears to huge bulbous pillars growing out of the rock face. Here and there, patches of crystal picked up the light and threw it back more brightly. Their way lay through a great hall of wonder, whose treasures had lain hidden for untold centuries. When they had passed, taking with them their small

104

light, the silence and blackness and desolation of the ages would drop back again, like a many-textured curtain.

Heather said, with awe, "Pity we can't take a photograph of all this."

"We can come back," Henry said, "after we've found our way out."

Peter said, "You were wrong about the water, Albrecht! You couldn't have anything drier than this."

Albrecht answered, "There are levels that are wet and others dry—is that not the case with caves, Henry?"

"They're called active systems and fossil systems," Henry said. "They've all been wet at some time. We've been lucky in getting into a fossil system."

"What happened to the water?" Heather asked. "It's not likely to come rolling back in a kind of tidal wave, is it?"

"I shouldn't think so. You do get sudden flows of water, but not in a fossil system. The water that used to flow through here has probably drained away to a lower level."

"But is it not so," Albrecht asked, "that there has been water also at a higher level, or there would not be stalactites in this cave?"

Henry held the light up, illuminating a jagged curtain of stalactites that hung from the arch of the cave wall.

"They're not active, either—not even from rain seepage. There's probably a belt of clay that diverts the rain to some other part."

"Rain, rain, stay away," Heather said. "Isn't it funny how different things feel when you have room to swing your arms about? Oh, look at those milky stalac-what's-its. Could I break a little one off?"

"I don't advise it," Henry said.

"No one's going to *miss* it, are they?"

"We shouldn't carry anything we don't absolutely have to."

"I said, a little one."

Henry looked at her. "Picture yourself crawling on your stomach through wet mud. So far we've been very lucky."

"Well, I could always abandon it. You don't know we're going to have to crawl through mud."

Henry shrugged. "Do as you think best."

She enlisted Peter's help in breaking off a mottled spear about two feet in length, which she pushed through the center of the coiled ladder. But she did not keep it for long. Shortly afterward they came on the first obstacle in the new chamber—a hill of rubble occupying the full width

105

of the cave. It had resulted, Henry explained, from a roof fall in the remote past.

Albrecht said, "It appears to rise up to the roof."

"It's not likely that it will," Henry said. "Anyway, we have to climb it to see."

"I'm dreadfully hungry," Heather complained.

"It's not time for supper yet."

"But we've been getting on so well—you said so."

"In which direction?" Cynthia asked.

"What do you mean—in which direction? Forward, of course."

Physical fatigue had added itself to the emotional lassitude in which Cynthia was caught up. She said wearily, "Apart from the way we got in, there may be another entrance to the caves—perhaps two. But we don't know where they are likely to be. We may be heading in the opposite direction to it, or them. There may only be a dead end in front of us."

"That's cheerful!" Heather commented.

Henry said, "At least, we're managing to stay above the water table. And the immediate problem is climbing over this lot."

"Without even a little snack?" Heather persisted.

"Yes."

The climb proved arduous and exhausting; the hill was made up very largely of loose stones, interspersed with awkwardly shaped boulders. At an early stage, Heather found that her stalactite spear was getting in the way and abandoned it. They struggled on, with the acetylene lamp throwing fantastic shadows from projecting spurs and pyramids of rock, their progress setting off small slides of stone in which one of them might drop back a painful ten feet or more. Before they had reached the crest, the lamp expired, and there was a delay while Henry re-charged it. While he was doing so, they sat huddled together on the slope. They were all hungry now, and all tired.

When the crest was reached, it did not show them a simple descent to an ordinary cave floor, but a dip followed by another rise beyond. They had to slither down into the hollow and then climb again, only to find the pattern repeated. This time the subsequent rise merged into a fairly level plateau, but still one made up of stone and loose rubble. Progress was slow, and there were many checks. They were still on the rubble when the lamp flickered again and went out.

106

Henry said, "It's after nine o'clock. That's the time I said we would rest for the night."

Heather said, "My God, yes, please! I'm ready to fall asleep as I stand."

Peter said, with a wan attempt at humor, "Don't you feel we ought to have the mattress changed? It's got rocks in it."

"You do not think we should go on a little?" Albrecht asked.

Henry had switched his headlamp on again. The light rested on Albrecht's face, outlining with brutal harshness the marks of his premature aging.

"No!" Heather said. "Anyone who goes on goes without me. I'm dead."

"It is a very long cave," Albrecht said, "but of course there must be an end to it."

His eyes were steady on the dimness of Henry's face under the light, and Henry stared back. There was something between the two men—something both had realized and both feared.

"The rest of you stop here," Henry said. "I'll recce on a bit. I'd like to get off this stuff if it's possible."

Peter said, "Let me go, for a change."

"No, stay. I won't be long."

As the noise of Henry's progress faded away from them. Cynthia realized what it was that he and Albrecht had been thinking of. All their hopes lay in discovering exits from the cave they were in, and these, in most cases, would be at floor level. They could have passed over half a dozen during their slow trek across the rubble plateau. If the plateau were to continue to the cave's end . . . then there would be nothing to do but go back—back through the rubble cave, down into the shallow cave beyond, and so into that drain-hole which must by now be a torrent of rushing water.

Heather said, "What about a light while we're waiting?"

Cynthia said, "No. We don't need it."

"We do, to divide supper up."

"It can wait until Henry comes back."

"I can't think why he had to go pushing on," Heather said. "It's not very comfortable here, but I don't suppose he'll find anything much better."

"Wait," Cynthia said, her voice breaking with tiredness. "We can wait."

Albrecht's hand touched her, and drew her in to lie beside him on the stones. She cuddled against him like a

107

child, aware only of the living friendliness of his body. He helped her to lie so that he cushioned her from much contact with the rubble, but they did not kiss. Something about it teased her memory, but she was too tired to formulate it effectively. She was drifting into sleep when the realization came quite suddenly, shocking her back into wakefulness: this was how her body formed itself to Henry's, in the comfort and sensual tiredness of their marriage bed.

They could hear Henry's return some distance away, but were all too tired and uninterested to call out to him. Cynthia reluctantly disengaged herself from Albrecht as the light danced nearer.

Henry said, "If you can manage a bit farther—we're nearly at the end of the rubble. A couple of hundred yards, that's all."

They picked themselves up, Heather protesting, and set off again under Henry's guidance. He did not bother to recharge the acetylene lamp, but allowed Peter to use his torch in place of his own headlamp. The going was just as hard, and their muscles as painful and reluctant, but at least there was the assurance that this particular stretch would soon be behind them. A hundred yards farther on, they found themselves on a downward slope.

Albrecht said quietly to Henry, "And the prospects?"

"Good." His voice was a little slurred with weariness. "At least two tunnels."

"We are having good fortune."

"Yes."

The slope dropped still more sharply, and Heather, losing her footing, slithered down the last few feet. Peter's light, which had been illuminating the ground immediately in front of them, was flashed forward to cover her. It revealed her sprawling on a frozen sea.

"Ice!" Peter exclaimed. "Is it a glacier?"

He went forward and helped Heather to her feet. Then he bent down and touched the surface with his hand.

"It's not ice—it's not cold enough."

Henry switched on his headlamp. "A stalagmite floor." He turned his head. "Look at the walls."

They were encrusted with crystals, multicolored and dazzling, flowers and swords and cobwebs, all jeweled. It was a display that paled the memory of everything they had seen before. They stood together, staring into the torchlight.

Heather said, in a quiet voice, "Do you remember Sin-

108

bad—the Valley of the Roc? That's how I always thought it would be."

"Would you like me to pluck a few out for you?" Peter asked. He glanced at Henry. "I can't pull that wall down, can I?"

"I hardly think so. But I shouldn't bother to take any all the same. There's no point in picking flowers when you've got to march across a desert immediately afterward."

Peter said buoyantly, "We must be over the worst of it now." He shone his own torch farther along; a handsome archway, high and wide, led out from the cave. "Plenty of scope."

Henry said, "Just as you like." His voice drooped with weariness. "I think this is a good place to have supper and lie up for the night. Do you think you could divide up, Sinner?"

Albrecht was lighting the acetylene lamp. In its brightness, the magic of their surroundings broadened and became more general, but was not lessened on that account. The cave here was some thirty feet across. The floor of frozen milk, flat, apart from an occasional corrugation of wave, ran without interruption between the walls. The whole shimmering palace of crystal stretched away to a point, only dimly visible, where the cave appeared to split into two separate branches. Nearer to them, on the other side, there was another exit tunnel, but smaller and less promising.

The great slope of rubble down which they had recently scrambled was a contrast pointing up the delicate beauty of the world of fragile crystal on which it impinged. Ahriman, Cynthia thought, and Ormuzd—the dark and the light. The recollection was a vagrant one; only the extremity of her tiredness, she felt, enabled her to remember the names. But she remembered the long-forgotten conversation and the picture she had had of darkness, palpable and massive, bearing down on and crushing the bright pinnacles of light. Now it was made real.

She took the haversack in which the food and the odd items like candles, spare batteries and boxes of matches were kept, and opened it. The store of provisions was pitifully small.

She asked Henry, "How much can we eat?"

He had to summon up his attention; he yawned heavily and shook his head.

"If we open one of the tins of meat, we can have half now and the other half before we set off again."

She took out the small tin of pressed beef and stared at it.

"Half—among five of us."

"Open the tin of biscuits and see how many there are."

She opened the tin. They were Osborne biscuits. She did not like them herself; Henry, on the other hand, had a sober passion for them and often took a tin with him when caving. Patiently she counted the biscuits. There were twenty-three.

Henry had been watching her count. He said, "One each, I think. And we can eat the small bar of chocolate as well."

Albrecht murmured, "That is twenty grams of praline to each of us."

"Seven-tenths of an ounce," Peter said. "Who gets the crumbs that fall from the table of this remarkable banquet?"

"Couldn't we finish off the tin of meat, at least?" Heather asked. "We're bound to find our way out tomorrow. Look how far we've come today—miles and miles."

Henry said, "There's enough food for just over four meals, on that ration. That means that forty-eight hours from now we'll only have the dried banana and the nuts and raisins; and the following morning we shan't have anything."

"Tomorrow night," Heather said, "we'll all be eating an enormous dinner."

"I hope you're right. Can you manage the tin, Sinner?"

Cynthia borrowed a knife from Albrecht to make the scrupulous division that was necessary. She divided the meat first, and handed the tiny mounds round, each bare mouthful resting on a biscuit. Then she tackled the chocolate praline bar. She had to cut across the ridges of the chocolate, and found herself with one piece fractionally larger than the other four. She gave it to Henry. He took it from her automatically; his eyes were on Peter and Heather.

He said, his voice suddenly sharp, "No! We're not going to have that kind of thing."

Cynthia saw Peter guiltily taking back the piece of chocolate he had been trying to pass surreptitiously to Heather.

"You don't think I would have taken it, do you?" Heather asked indignantly.

Peter said, "I'd rather she had it, Henry. I'm so damn tired I've lost my appetite. I really don't want it."

110

Henry said, "Eat it." After a moment, Peter put the piece of chocolate in his mouth and began to chew. There was an awkward silence.

Henry said, "You wouldn't have been helping Heather by giving her that piece of chocolate, Peter. We may find our way out to the open tomorrow; but if we don't, we're going to start feeling the strain—even if the going is as easy as it has been up to now. There's going to be a very heavy drain on our energies, and the ration of food we can afford doesn't go a long way toward replacing it. We've got to be able to keep going—all of us. If one person breaks down, it endangers everyone else. Do you understand that?"

Peter said, "I'm stronger than Heather. I could go without more easily."

"The stronger you are," Henry said wearily, "the more you need to replace energy. I want you to promise that you will eat your full ration, as long as the food lasts."

Heather said, "I'll see that he does. Can we have a drink of water, if someone's got a thimble?"

He passed her the water bottle. "You'll have to gauge what's a mouthful." He glanced at Albrecht. "You were wrong about the water, weren't you?"

Albrecht nodded. "Yes. Do you think that is a bad thing?"

"I hope not." Henry rummaged in the haversack again. "One cigarette each, I think. I don't need to tell you to keep the stubs, I imagine."

"One whole cigarette!" Heather marveled.

Henry doused the lamp, and Albrecht offered around his lighter. Its small yellow flame spired against the blackness that once more pressed close about them. Then the lighter, in its turn, was put out, leaving only the flickering red points, briefly flaring up and dying, of their cigarettes.

Peter said, "I suppose people will be searching for us by now."

"That is certain," Albrecht said.

"We couldn't make some sort of signal to them, I suppose?" Heather asked hopefully. "Knock on the walls, or something?"

Henry said, "There's absolutely no hope of our being rescued from outside. We must all realize that."

Heather said, "I know you're the expert, Henry, but do you have to be quite so gloomy? What harm would it do if we were expecting to be rescued, even if it didn't happen?"

"Everything depends on our own efforts. If we were to

111

slacken up the least bit in the hope of someone else doing things for us, it might be enough to finish us off. People have died in caves within a few feet of a way out."

"That may be true," Albrecht said, "but it does no harm to say that for the present we have done well. Is that not true also?"

"Yes. We're all alive, unhurt, dry; and we have several possibilities when we start again in the morning. That's a lot more than we could have reasonably hoped for just after the fall. Now we need to get some sleep."

"On a marble slab?" Heather asked. "I don't think I've got the right anatomy for it."

Peter said, "On the contrary, I should think you're better equipped than the rest of us—than Henry, Albrecht and me, at any rate."

"We'll be able to rest, at least," Henry said. "If we are tired enough, we'll sleep as well. I don't have much doubt that we will. The thing to do is to huddle together for maximum warmth. The ladies had better have the inside berths."

"Where," inquired Heather, "is the bathroom?"

"All I can suggest," Henry said, "is the opposite side of the cave. We can take it in turns with Albrecht's torch."

Albrecht switched on the torch; its light was comparatively feeble. He said, "The battery is almost finished."

"It will do," Henry said, "for our present purposes."

Cynthia lay on the smooth expanse of stalagmite, with Heather on one side of her and Henry on the other. She was able to tell, from the deeper regularity of her breathing, that Heather had fallen asleep quite soon. Henry, she thought, was asleep as well.

She was aware of a coldness, less physical than emotional, which kept her own mind from rest, despite her body's weariness. She knew what caused it: not simply the foreboding of death, but the consciousness of isolation, making death more terrible. She had thought the warm pressure of Henry and Heather, on either side, might allay the chill of loneliness as it did the physical chill, but it did not happen. After a time, she felt her body beginning to shiver—not violently, but uncontrollably.

Henry's voice whispered behind her ear. "Sinner!"

"Yes?"

"Don't be afraid. We're going to be all right. I've got a feeling about it."

112

She made no answer. He rubbed his hand over her side. "Tomorrow night we'll be back in bed at the inn."

She still did not reply, and Henry did not say anything else. Soon she felt the small involuntary jerk of his leg which was the sign that he, too, had fallen asleep. But she had stopped shivering, and after a time her own consciousness began to fade. She drifted into a dream in which Henry and Albrecht were trying to persuade her to come into the swimming pool at the *Schloss*. There was hot brilliant sunshine, and they splashed water at her in strands of gleaming crystal. She tried desperately hard to tell them that the appearances were false, that really they were all trapped underground in a cave, but they would not listen to her. They only laughed, and splashed the warm blue water.

SHE WAS AWAKENED by Heather, shifting uneasily against her, and shortly afterwards Peter coughed. Heather whispered something to him, and he whispered back. She moved her own legs, which were cramped, and felt Henry yield behind her. She turned her head and said quietly, "What time is it?"

"Half past three."

Heather said, with relief, "You're awake as well, then. Does anybody mind if I sit up and stretch?"

Henry said, "I think we're all awake. I take it no one wants to lie on in bed?"

Heather sat up and Cynthia could feel her wriggling her body vigorously. Heather said, "I never knew I had so many muscles. I feel absolutely black and blue." She sounded, however, quite cheerful about it.

There was a distinct note of cheerfulness also in Henry's voice, when he replied, "A brisk walk will make all the difference."

He twisted around to reach his helmet and switched on the light. The world of scintillating crystal sprang once more into life about them.

"I think we could light the lamp," Henry added. "By you, I believe, Albrecht. And then breakfast."

It was difficult not to respond to some extent to the general lift of emotions. The five or six hours uneasy slumber, Cynthia felt, had done more than restore energy; by dividing them off from the time immediately following the rock fall, it had given them the chance of looking at things freshly. For the first time since she had stood in the river chamber, she did not feel the certainty of death. They were all alive and well. The hill, it was clear, was honeycombed with tunnels and caves. There was no reason why they should not find their way out.

She said, as Albrecht lit the acetylene lamp, "What do we have for breakfast—the same as we had for supper?"

Henry glanced at her and smiled; she read his awareness, gleaned from the tone of her voice, of her new optimism.

He said, "Yes. The same. The rest of the beef, a biscuit, and half of one of the blocks of chocolate."

Heather said. "I'm thirsty."

"We must still go easy on water," Henry warned. "We aren't sure of finding any."

"A cup of tea?" Heather said wistfully. "I suppose one ought not to start thinking about it."

It did not take them long to complete the meal—the sharing out took far more time than the consuming—and they set off, under Henry's guidance, in a resumption of exploration.

Cynthia found herself beside Albrecht, and put her hand out to his. Their fingers pressed together; and once more the contact meant something more than merely the reassurance of flesh warm against flesh. She lagged a little further behind, and put her face up to him in the gloom, and they kissed, briefly but with passion.

He whispered to her, "Ah, Cynthia!"

As, reluctantly, she parted from him, she wondered about that: it had sounded almost like an appeal.

Henry decided to try the two tunnels before going on to the point where the cave divided, and he led them to the smaller entrance first. To begin with, it was possible to walk in it, bending low, but the roof tilted sharply downward, and after a few yards they were crawling.

After another few yards, Henry told the others to halt.

"It's a rat hole," he said. "It will be a tight crawl. Hold on here while I try it."

"What do we do?" Peter inquired, "if you get stuck?"

"Don't worry. I won't."

The four of them huddled together, watching Henry ease himself down onto his side and begin a wriggling

114

progress under the narrowing slit of rock. His headlamp threw light ahead. but his body prevented them from seeing anything but an intermittent glow.

. "Good job we've got Henry with us," Peter observed. "We'd be in a mess without him."

"He does all the work," Heather said, "and we just lie cozily squashed together here and wait."

Peter said, "He's coming back."

He flashed his torch, and they saw that Henry was wriggling back toward them. As, at last, he twisted himself around to face them, Peter asked, "No good?"

"Not this one," Henry said. "When I couldn't get any farther, I got my arm fully· extended in front of me. I didn't touch an end, but it makes no odds. If there is. a way, we haven't got the equipment to·get through."

They began a general movement of retreat.

"Never mind," Heather said cheerfully. "Plenty more to try."

They crossed the cave's milky floor to the large archway they had seen. It was crusted with jewels of many-colored crystals. The tunnel beyond provided easy walking; they were able to go two or three abreast.

Henry's warning was abrupt: "Hold it!"

They stopped. Looking more closely, it was possible to see that the headlamp lit up a darker, unreflecting gloom before them. The light crept nearer as Henry dropped his head. It shone on a rounded edge, surrounding emptiness and blackness.

"I nearly missed that,"˥Henry said soberly. "Bring up · the lamp. Albrecht. We'd better have a look at it."

The drop extended across the entire width of the gallery which, it became clear, was actually a lateral shaft opening · out at some point in the face of a great cliff. Beyond the upper lip, above their heads, the light picked out. a vertical rise as smooth and apparently illimitable as the precipice beneath. From very far below, there came the muted rumble of rushing water.

Peter whistled. "If one of us had tumbled over that . . . Don't you think we ought to be roped together, Henry?"

Henry said, "If one of us had ,gone, there would have been four left. With- experiencéd climbers, a lifeline is worth while—they've developed the instinct of· reacting properly against a sudden pull. With us . . . one over might mean five over."

"There is no hope of crossing this?" Albrecht asked.

Henry peered out into the beam of light. "I think that's

115

the other side we can see. But that doesn't mean to say there's another shaft there; and even if there were, we've no way of getting over."

Peter looked down over the cliff edge; Heather, with an indignant shudder, drew him back.

"Mightn't it be worth while going down on a ladder?" Peter asked. "I don't mind having a shot."

Heather exclaimed, "Oh, no you won't!"

"Down that," Henry asked, "with a thirty-foot ladder?"

"We could tie the two ladders together—tie a rope on as well, if necessary."

Henry bent down and picked up a loose stone. He weighed it in his hand for a moment, before tossing it out over the cliff. They listened; no sound came up above the distant roar of the torrent.

"You wouldn't hear it enter the water, anyway," Peter argued. "The stream's too noisy."

"Possibly not. But that tells us the drop goes sheer for a long way down. This is where we turn back again. We might have to try it, but I'd rather try something else first."

It was curious, Cynthia thought as they trailed back towards the main cave, that no one seemed particularly depressed by this second setback of the new day. There was even an impression of relief when they came out under the arch and on the white translucent stalagmite floor.

Peter said cheerfully, "Back on the main line! Full steam ahead now."

As they approached the point where the cave forked, Albrecht said, "Which way? To right or left?"

Henry was in advance of the rest. He said, "I don't think it matters."

"Why not?" Peter began. "Oh, I see. . . ."

They could all see. The fork did not represent any true division; it was simply a rock pillar dividing the cave temporarily into two halves. Several yards farther on, the two courses rejoined.

They advanced along the right-hand course. They were still walking on a smooth, dully shining stalagmite floor, but over toward the side of the cave there was now an outcrop of frosted crystal bushes. It was as though they walked, by lantern light at night, over a frozen lake edged with ice-heavy vegetation. One might almost expect some water bird to rise with loud flapping wings into a starry sky. But this was a lifeless world apart from themselves, its meridian a savage weight of rock.

116

The ground began to dip. More ominously, the cave itself narrowed; walls pressed closer, the jagged roof sagged down. They went on in silence, their new optimism overlaid by the consciousness that their little world was closing in on them with every forward step. The descent became steeper, and Albrecht, the tallest of the three men, had to stoop slightly.

There was a crackling sound. Peter said, "Blast!"

They halted. Henry asked, "What's the matter?"

One of his feet had gone through the stalagmite layer, which was fractured like ice. Water dripped from his rubber boot. The hole which remained after he had regained level footing brimmed with clear green-blue water.

"Too thin for skating," Heather said. "I'd better tread carefully. It means wet feet if I go through."

"Here's your chance to quench that thirst, Heather," Henry said.

She said, in mock outrage, "What? Where Petey's been washing his hulking feet?"

Henry took the haversack and, bending down, took out the water bottle. He removed the cork and dipped the bottle beneath the water. Bubbles of air disturbed its icy clearness.

He said as he straightened up, "Water again. I didn't think I would be so glad to see it."

"Perhaps," Albrecht suggested, "we will see more than we wish."

Henry stoppered the bottle. "We shan't die of thirst, at any rate."

They continued on their way through the still narrowing cave—it had become little better than a tunnel. All at once, around a bend, it opened out again, and the false ice of the stalagmite floor abruptly ended. It gave way to a level blackness that appeared to have no limits. Henry stopped, and they automatically followed his lead.

"After all this time," he said, "a lake at last."

"A lake?" Heather said. "That's not water!"

"Try and walk on it," Henry suggested. He unstrapped the rubber boat from his back and began gently to unfold it. "At least I haven't carried this for nothing."

Heather and Peter crowded forward to examine more closely the surface of the lake. Heather dipped her fingers in it and, after licking one, stooped down, cupped her hands, and drank.

Albrecht said to Henry, "You have said that the boat will carry two. You will go yourself first—and who else?"

117

"You, I thought. The rest will have to wait while we see what the lake offers."

Albrecht nodded. "How shall we be sure of returning to this place? We have no way of marking our path."

Henry had the boat uncreased and was beginning to inflate it. He paused to get his breath back and replied, "We certainly shan't try any Columbus stunts of sailing out over the rim of the world. The obvious thing to do is hug one of the shores. If we keep on bearing to the left, and make a note of all the tunnels, we only have to count them off on the way back."

He gave his attention once more to the task of inflation.

Peter said, "Do you think there would be any fish in a stretch of water like this?"

"Sometimes, I think," Albrecht said. "But they are white and blind. They do not need either color or eyes."

"Anyway," Heather said, "we've got nothing to cook them with if we caught any."

"I have an idea," Peter said, "that I'm just about hungry enough to eat them raw. But I don't see how one would go about catching them. Once, when I was in Ireland, I went salmon fishing with lanterns—you know, spearing them as they came up to the light. It wouldn't work if they're blind, though, would it?"

Henry paused, gasping. "You seem to have a lot of breath, Peter," he said. "You can take over the job of blowing up the boat."

"Darling," Heather said, "I did tell you you talked too much."

"If that's what we're going on," Peter said, "this is a woman's job—yours, my sweetie."

Heather backed away. "Oh, no!"

Peter grabbed at her and they wrestled. She abandoned resistance suddenly, and the pair of them came crashing to the ground. They landed almost on top of Henry who was still crouched over the boat. There was a moment of confusion and Heather's giggling, before Henry spoke. His voice was bitter and unpleasant. "The next time you two do something like that, you can do the rest of the journey on your own."

Peter said, "Sorry, Henry."

Henry stared at him angrily. "That's very nice. Are you apologizing for anything in particular, or just to make the party go?"

"He's apologizing," Heather said, "so as not to upset you. I think he's overdoing it."

118

Henry waited for a time, his gaze now on Heather, before replying. He said, "We're down here because you two played the fool. It's only a matter of luck that we're not drowned. Just now you endangered us for a second time. There'd better not be a third."

Heather said contemptuously, "I suppose we might have fallen on you and broken your neck—is that what you call endangering people?"

Henry held up the half-inflated boat. "I was talking about this. It's made of rubber, and not very thick rubber, either. I haven't got a repair kit. And if it's pressed against a sharp edge of rock, it can be gashed in an instant."

His eyes were still on her. "Well?" Heather made no reply. "Do you feel like going back up to the cave and trying your luck down that drop to the river? Because that's the only alternative we have if we're prevented from taking to the water."

Peter said, "We're sorry, Henry. We will be careful from now on."

"If you're not," Henry said, "we separate. There's a limit to the amount I'm going to risk the necks of the rest of us on your account." He stood up. "Now carry on with blowing it up."

There was no further comment from anyone. Peter and Heather squatted down together, and Peter went on with the inflation of the rubber boat. Henry began to rummage in the haversack.

"We'd better have a few candles and a waterproofed box of matches with us, to be on the safe side. And I'll take a spare battery for my headlamp. I'm not sure how long the present one will last, but I doubt if it's got more than an hour's life in it."

"Are we to take the acetylene lamp as well?" Albrecht inquired.

"Yes. And we'd better have a spare charge."

Cynthia asked, "How long do you think you will be gone?"

Henry shrugged. "There's no way of telling in advance. It depends what we find, and how soon we find it." He turned to Peter and said cheerfully, "How is it coming along?"

Peter took his mouth away from the tube, and paused to get his breath back. "Nearly up." He handed it to Heather. "You have a go." To Henry, he continued, "Are you taking any of the gear with you—ladders, irons and stuff?"

119

"No."

"Mightn't you need them?"

"Not on this trip." He paused and looked at Cynthia. "This question of time—we'd better fix an end limit. Make it six hours. We should be back in four at the outside, and we'll turn back after two hours, whatever the results. But we'd better allow the extra couple of hours in case we run into unforeseen difficulties on the return journey."

Cynthia asked dryly, "And after six hours?"

"You will have to backtrack and try that cliff." His eyes turned to Peter. "Make sure your irons are well dug in— at an acute angle to the direction of strain. And, for God's sake, go carefully."

Heather gave a loud whoosh of relief and held the boat up for Henry's inspection. He took it from her with great care and carried it over to the water's edge. He waded in two or three feet—the water came halfway up to his knees —and placed downward pressure on the boat, his head-lamp brightly illuminating that part of the water around the boat where, if there were a leak, bubbles could be expected to show.

"All right, I hope."

There was a short mooring rope attached to a ring on the inflated bulwarks. Henry came back to dry land, holding the end of this.

He said, "Ready when you are, Albrecht. Have you got the paddles?"

Albrecht gave him the solid rubber paddles, and then made the rounds, shaking hands with Peter, Heather and Cynthia, in the Continental fashion. Heather giggled a little. Cynthia felt the warm pressure of his fingers and had a moment's panic fear that she would never see him again —that perhaps Henry, suspecting the truth, would use his experience to kill Albrecht, or leave him trapped somewhere. . . .

She realized the absurdity and melodramatic quality of that when Henry came to kiss her goodbye. He held her lightly and said, "Look after yourself, darling. It won't be long before we're back."

The two men waded out to the boat together. Henry got in first and steadied it while Albrecht climbed in after him. They waved, and then started to paddle. The acetylene lamp, although it had been taken with them, was doused; the only light was the beam from Henry's headlamp, cutting a swath through the darkness in front of the boat.

120

Heather said, "Well, I supose we'd best make ourselves comfy. What's the best way of passing the time?"

"I knew two blokes once," Peter said, "who could play mental chess. They didn't need light or a board or pieces."

"Dolt!" Heather said affectionately.

"Mind you," Peter said, "they generally used to start arguing after seven or eight moves. What about telling ghost stories?"

It was rather more than two hours later that Cynthia caught the first gleam of light, away to their left. She told the other two, and they all watched its approach. The beam of light moved along the verge of the lake, lighting up the glistening walls and, at last, fixing on the little stalagmite beach on which they sat.

Heather called out, "Here we are. What's the news?"

As the little boat was paddled toward them they saw that it held only one man now. In Cynthia, momentarily, the absurd irrational fear sprang up again; then she saw that it was Albrecht, wearing Henry's helmet with the lamp on it. He clambered over the side several yards from the shore, and led the boat in behind him.

"Henry's found a place then?" Peter asked.

"Yes. He has stayed behind."

"What's it like?"

"There is clay there—and mud."

Heather said dolefully, "And me in shoes. What's good about that?"

"It leads upward," Albrecht said. "The clay and mud have perhaps been washed down by the rains—from outside."

"Jolly good," Peter said. "I suppose the idea is, we go one at a time. Ladies first?"

"No. Henry desires you to come with me now. Then you can help him at that end. There are side tunnels to be explored, and in one place climbing. We are to take the ropes and irons on this trip."

"Must you go?" Heather said. "I suppose you must. Darling, what time is it?"

"Nearly nine o'clock."

She groaned. "Oh—breakfast!"

The two women watched the boat disappear again. The sense of loneliness was intensified.

Heather said, "Cyn, you don't mind if I snuggle up against you?"

"Snuggle away. Has it occurred to you that one of us will have to stay here alone, on the next trip?"

Heather jerked in sudden horrified realization, and her elbow caught Cynthia in the ribs. She gave a small gasp of pain.

Heather said, "Darling, I'm sorry! You gave me a shock. I can't possibly stay here by myself—I'd just go roaring, raving mad."

"That leaves me, then," Cynthia said.

"Would you?"

"I suppose I'll have to."

Heather felt for her hand, and squeezed it gratefully. "I do admire you, Cyn. I'm a bit scared of you, too."

"Why on earth?"

"I don't know, really. I suppose perhaps it's because you don't generally say much and you always seem to be in command of things, while with me it's the other way round."

"I think you're misjudging yourself," Cynthia told her. "Look at the situation we're in now—you've been the most cheerful and optimistic of the lot of us."

"That's because it seems more of a lark than anything else."

"A lark! Haven't you realized that right from the beginning the odds have been against our getting out alive? That they still are?"

"I haven't got much imagination, I suppose," Heather said apologetically. "I don't like being in the dark, but as long as there's someone with me it's not too bad. I didn't like it when we were going through that passage that kept on getting narrower and narrower, but apart from that I've not really minded."

"You've really not worried at all about it?"

"Well, I don't like being hungry, and not being able to wash properly, and all that."

"Nothing else?"

"Only that I hope we get out within a couple of days."

"Because we'll be starving if we don't?"

"No—the date. You know."

Cynthia laughed, and heard its hollow reverberation from the blackness all round them. "If only that was the worst we had to worry about!"

When Albrecht had taken Heather, Cynthia was faced with the actuality of loneliness. He had left a torch with her, and at first she flashed it now and then on her surroundings, as a means of reassurance. But, after several surveys of this kind, she stopped doing it. There was no

122

change—there could be no change, As far as she knew, the walls that enclosed the great lake, the lake itself, the thin crust of stalagmite on which she sat, had not changed in centuries and would not change for countless centuries to come. There was no sun or frost to bleach or crack these stones, no wind to flick the motionless black waters, no dust to abrade, over the years, the jagged spurs of rock. In this dark pocket under the earth the only time that passed was that marking the minutes and seconds of her own life. She alone lived and breathed and slowly moved along the chain of her mortality toward a known inevitable end.

In addition to the light, she glanced frequently, in the first hour, at the luminous dial of her wrist watch, and marveled at the slow progress of the hand around the dial. Several times she lifted the watch to her ear to make sure that it was ticking. But in the second hour she fell into a reverie of childhood memories. She darted from scene to sunlit scene in her mind and at last embarked on the reliving of one particular summer day in the country. She was shaken out of it unexpectedly by the flash of light from the water. She flashed the torch in return, and a few moments later saw Albrecht paddling the little boat toward her.

She got to her feet as he waded to the shore. He tied the end of the mooring rope to a rock projection. She stood waiting for him. The light from the helmet, as he moved toward her, was blinding.

She whispered, "Turn that off."

He did so, and she went into his arms.

She said, "Darling, darling Albrecht!"

"You have been very brave," he said, "to stay behind here by yourself."

She murmured into his ear, "Don't I get a reward for that?"

Guilty lovers, she thought, seek the dark, but surely none before had found a darkness so complete, an isolation so sure, so safe a private place. In the deep silence, they were aware of each tremor of the other's breath. And wanting him, it seemed, even more than she had done before, she was at the same time aware, with surprise and joy, of how much he wanted her. For the first time, in all their meetings, she felt that her own desire was matched and overpowered by a still stronger one.

The new landing place was a broad littoral of splintered

123

rocks, leading up a slope toward an egg-shaped cave. Albrecht carried the boat carefully over the broken ground toward the higher level. After all their journeying over hard or gravelly surfaces, Cynthia was surprised to find her feet sinking in, to some extent, as she walked. She mentioned it to Albrecht.

"This is the clay," he said. "If you touch it, you will find it is damp. It has been under water not a long while ago. Henry thinks there is a stream which from time to time brings clay and mud down here from the surface."

"Where are they now?" she asked.

Albrecht knelt down to deflate the boat and fold it up. "Henry has been seeking to trace the main course of the stream. There is a cave up here, and a climb. We will find them there."

"And then, perhaps, soon, we'll be out of the caves?" She could not see much of his face, as it was behind the light. She felt, however, that his voice showed some surprise at the optimism of her remark.

He said, "We must hope so. But it may still be very hard."

She said, "Yes, I know." But she did not believe now that anything could go wrong. "Kiss me—before we go and find them."

The climb Albrecht had spoken of proved a fairly simple one. The rock, against which the ladder swung, was wet and slimy. Peter helped her over the top; Heather and Henry were there, and the acetylene lamp was burning.

They were in a tunnel, about six feet wide and almost as high. The floor was silted in places with mud, but in others the bare bones of rock showed through. She could see that the tunnel ran straight, on a slightly upward incline, for twenty or thirty feet.

Heather said, "Here at last. I suppose we couldn't have another tiny snack before setting off again?"

"It's only just after one o'clock," Henry pointed out.

"But we've been up since half past three!"

Henry looked more exhausted than ever; the lines of strain and fatigue were more deeply graven on his face.

He said, "Perhaps we'll knock off a bit earlier—sixish, maybe. But I don't want us to hang about here any longer than is necessary. If this is an intermittent stream, it may start to flow again without warning. It's going to be a great deal easier to travel up a dry course than a wet one."

"We may be out by six," Heather objected.

Henry smiled slightly. "May."

"Petey, darling," Heather said, "show Cynthia and Albrecht what you found."

Peter produced something from his pocket and held it out into the light. It was a small broken twig, with a green leaf still attached to it. They all stared at it with an almost disbelieving fascination. Here was something, that had come down from the world of light and life to this grim underworld of darkness; every vein on the leaf breathed hope.

"If we're all ready," Henry said, "we'll travel."

For a time, the going was fairly easy, but after about a quarter of an hour the tunnel widened and dipped a little, and they found themselves confronted with a stretch of soft and fairly deep mud. Heather balked immediately at the prospect of wading through it and demanded that Peter carry her. As a result, progress, which was slow and difficult for all of them, their feet with each footstep having to be dragged out of the glutinous black ooze, was particularly arduous for him. When they got to the point where the mud gave way again to rock, he was completely exhausted.

Henry allowed them to rest for five minutes before continuing. They did so to the accompaniment of a distant whispering which was soon magnified into the unmistakable roar of rushing water.

"We must move fast," Henry urged. "That sounds like a lot of water. If it comes down here—or a good part of it —we're in trouble."

"Why should it come down here?" Peter asked.

"If the storms are continuing outside, then there could be sudden flooding. That might be the sort of thing that brings the mud down this passage. Water levels can rise a dozen feet in as many minutes."

Heather said, "But this tunnel isn't a dozen feet high."

"No. And it's getting lower."

The tunnel was narrowing into little better than a conduit; it was as though they had crawled up a bottle and were now reaching the neck. Soon they were down on hands and knees, with the ribbed roof scraping their backs and the noise of the angry flood growing continually louder.

Henry flicked on his headlamp. He said, "You'll have to douse the acetylene lamp again. It's a squeeze from here on. The idea is that you lie on one side and wriggle your way forward. You'll get the hang of things. The important thing is not to panic—if you do everything slowly and deliberately, you can't get stuck. Push the gear in front of you as you go."

Heather said, "I can't!" Fear had cut into the usual robust cheerfulness of her voice. "I really can't."

"We're nearly there," Henry said. "It can't be more than a few feet. I'll push through first, and help you through from the other end."

The sound of his reptant advance was barely audible above the noise of the water. They had no idea how far he had gone when a light flashed back toward them.

He called, "I'm through. You come first, Heather. I'll help you. Just take it easy. Easy, now."

Without the assurance and confidence that Henry offered, it would have been a terrifying passage through that narrow pipe of rock into the widening thunder of unseen water. As it was, they managed without much difficulty, but Heather, going forward too impetuously, slipped and fell. Cynthia heard her cry out, "Oh, my ankle!"

Henry asked urgently, "Can you stand on it?"

She uttered a small expression of discomfort. "I'm not sure . . . Yes, just about."

"You'll be all right in a minute or two. You've only turned it."

Cynthia herself was helped out of the hole. As Henry attended to the two men, she looked about her.

They stood on a ledge of rock, poised over the very edge of a waterfall. One end of the ledge was almost level with the river, seven or eight feet wide, which rushed toward a fall stretching from side to side. At the other end, the ledge hung perhaps twelve feet above the cold caldron into which the fall emptied. Peter flashed his torch and she saw that there was a bubbling pool of water, roughly circular and twenty or thirty feet in diameter, which appeared to find an outlet on the far side. The water foamed away under an arch of rock that did not seem to rise more than inches clear of it.

The ledge offered no other possibilities—the rock roof was about a foot above Albrecht's head.

Heather said, fear still naked in her voice, "After all that, we're stuck here. There's nowhere to go."

The light from Henry's headlamp swept across the waters. "It's not quite that bad," he said. "Look over there."

They followed his gesture. Several yards upstream, on the other side, there was a ledge a few feet above water level. Once their eyes had grown accustomed to tracing its

126

outline, it was possible to see that it continued, although sharply narrowing, to a point almost opposite them.

"But we can't get across there," Heather said.

"I wouldn't say that."

Henry took one of the ropes and began tying it securely around his waist.

Albrecht said, "You plan to cross? But it is a swift river and may be deep."

"I don't think it will be deep right on the edge of the fall. And I'm relying on you to keep a firm hold of the end of the rope and pull me up if I go over. When I get across, I'll try to fix my end of the line about four feet above the water level. If you do the same with the other end here, Albrecht, that will give us a holding line for Peter and the ladies. I'll have to ask you to come over on an ordinary lifeline, though, if we're going to be able to salvage the other rope."

As soon as he stepped off the ledge, the water foamed up around his boots, but it did not foam very high. The river, as it approached the lip of the fall, was not more than a foot deep. Henry grinned back at them triumphantly before continuing to cross. He made each step a careful test of the footing ahead, bracing himself against the savage sideways pull of the river. At one point they saw him throw up his arms to keep a balance, and they tightened their grips on the rope. But he recovered, and two or three steps farther saw him across and clambering onto the narrow ledge there.

He pulled more of the rope over and, precariously poised, twisted it round a jutting spear of rock. Then, his back against the rock face, he inched his way along the ledge to the place where it broadened to traversable dimensions. He had two irons with him, and they saw him using one to hammer the other in as a belaying pin. When he had finished, a line of rope ran across the fall and then up-river.

Meanwhile, Albrecht had hammered an iron into the rock face above the ledge. He said, "That makes all ready. We must now tie the other rope round our waists as a lifeline, and then we can go."

Peter asked Heather, "How's your ankle? I suppose I'd better carry you across?"

"Yes, please." She added anxiously, "You can, can't you?"

"Yes. You get on the lifeline and you can hang onto me while I trip across by the holding line."

127

Albrecht said, "It is best that all should be tied on the lifeline."

"Not practicable if I'm carrying Heather," Peter said. "Either there will be too much slack between us, in which case the rope is likely to trip me up; or we shall be tied too close together to be able to maneuver when we reach the other side. As long as Heather is on the line, you don't need to worry about me. She won't let go in a hurry."

Albrecht said doubtfully, "I am not sure that is right."

Heather had tied the rope around her waist. "O.K.," she said. "All aboard."

She clambered onto Peter's back and settled herself. He stepped out into the river, holding the rope which Henry had strung across the fall. He and Heather were picked out in the light from the acetylene lamp and, less effectively, by the beam from Henry's headlamp.

They moved steadily across. Once or twice, Peter paused to make sure of his footing. But they were nearly at the other side when he fell.

It happened very quickly, and without the others' being able to make out much of what had happened; they were at the point in the crossing where the light, from either source, was least effective. A stone must have turned under his foot. They saw him stagger backward. He appeared to let go of the holding line to try and get his balance, just as Heather clutched at it for support. In a moment he had fallen over the foaming lip of the waterfall. Heather fell at the same time, but one rope held her and she held the other. She stood teetering on the very edge, the water washing round her legs, looking down with terror into the caldron.

They saw Peter come to the surface of the furious water. He was making some attempt to sustain himself against its buffeting. But his efforts were feeble. Albrecht quickly took the electron ladder from Cynthia and began to unroll it. Heather looked to see what they were doing, made some undistinguishable cry, and looked back to where Peter was struggling. The caldron was carrying him toward the outlet.

Cynthia said, "She's untying herself from the lifeline!"

Albrecht had uncoiled the ladder, and now threw one end down to dangle in the churning pool. As he did so, Cynthia saw that Heather had freed herself from the rope. She stood briefly, one hand on the holding line, and then dived off the edge into the pool below.

It was difficult to see things very clearly in the light

128

from the acetylene lamp. A swirl in the water looked as though it might be Heather coming to the surface, but when Cynthia looked more closely the swirl had vanished. She could see Peter, though. He struggled with increasing weakness, against the current pulling him on. When he reached the outlet, he tried to raise himself to hold onto the rock face, in a last attempt to survival. His fingers clutched at the low arch for perhaps a second, and then were gone.

Cynthia turned away. She felt Albrecht's arm on her shoulders.

She said, "And Heather?"

"She also, I am afraid."

The roar of the waters had the merciless drumming insistence that was, she remembered, like the sound of German bombers during the war. It was something that must be faced before it unnerved her completely. She turned around. "The rope is still all right?"

"Yes. But do you not wish to wait a little, until you are better from the shock?"

"No. I'll go now."

She stepped out and felt the vicious undertow as the water whipped toward its plunge. Foot by foot she advanced, her hands on the holding line. Halfway across, a compulsion took her, and she looked down into the frothing tortured depths. She swayed a little and then, her eyes on the rock face ahead, continued to cross. Her movements did not seem to be co-ordinated by her brain; she was conscious of nothing but the twisting weight of water against her legs and its unchanging triumphant thunder.

There was a sensation of lightness and freedom as she moved out of the water to clamber along the last section of the rope, feeling for the small foothold afforded by the ledge. But as Henry reached down to help her up, the noise of the water dinned in her ears, a beast fed but still unsatisfied.

10.

SHE SAT UNMOVING, her back against the rock face, while Henry watched Albrecht's passage over the top of the fall and at last helped him up to the wider part of the ledge.

She heard Henry say to Albrecht, "What happened? I couldn't see very well."

"He lost his footing. When he fell, he perhaps hurt himself. I threw down the ladder but he could not reach it. Then Heather unloosed herself from the lifeline and dived in. I think she saw the ladder and was going to try to help him to reach it."

"And then?"

"She did not come to the surface. Perhaps she hit her head on a rock below the water. I think she was probably carried away even before he was."

"Why did you let him go unroped?"

"He said that, carrying Heather, it would have been too difficult."

Henry said bitterly, "Yes, she couldn't be allowed to get her feet wet. As a result, he drowns himself and her."

Cynthia spoke at last. She said in weary protest, "They're dead. Isn't that enough?"

"It should have been," Henry said, "but it isn't. They have to cut down what slender chances we have, as well."

"How? What are you talking about?"

"Only that Heather had the haversack."

"Oh." She looked down at the dark restless waters. "The food . . ."

He said impatiently, "We can do without the food. It's light I'm concerned about. The spare batteries and acetylene charges were in that pack, and most of the candles and matches. I've got a couple of candles and a box of matches in my pocket. There's perhaps an hour's charge in the acetylene lamp, and double that in my headlamp. What do you think about your torch, Albrecht?"

"Not long, I think. Less than an hour."

"We'd better try to save the acetylene lamp as long as possible." He doused the lamp, and they were in pitch

130

darkness for a moment before he flicked on the light on his helmet. "We'll have to do everything we can to economize. As a matter of fact, I think your torch is most easily expendable, Albrecht." He turned his headlamp off again. "Try to use it in short bursts. For the time being, you lead, and we'll come after as best we can. Cynthia's still roped—you tie yourself on the line in front and I'll do the same behind."

"You wish us to be on a lifeline?"

"Yes. From now on, as long as we're on the move."

"What's different now?" Cynthia asked.

"Two things. One is that we've lost the ones who were most likely to drag everybody over a cliff; and I think I could take the strain on you two."

His callous dismissal of their deaths was more brutal than his earlier anger had been, but she felt that she herself had lost the power to react in any way approaching normal.

She said, "And the other?"

"I was worried in case I myself slipped—it takes some experience to meet the kind of strain you get. As it is . . ." He paused, and she could visualize him smiling slightly in the darkness. "If I go, it means taking with me one of the two torches, the two candles, and the matches. Your chances of getting out will be small if that happens. Even smaller than they are at present."

For the moment, there was nothing between them but the lunatic logic of common sense; words to the violent tune of the river plunging into rocky deeps.

She said, "You could share out the candles."

"And the matches, too? Candles aren't much good without matches; and matches need a box to be struck on. And waterproofing."

"Albrecht has his lighter."

"Yes. I'd forgotten that. Then you'd better have one of the candles. Here. Something else as well."

The candle was pushed into her hand, and she automatically put it in a pocket. The second object was roughly cylindrical and of metal. She recognized it after a while.

"Your knife!"

"It has a good edge. Good enough for nylon."

"By why give it to me?"

"You may need it. You're Number Two on the rope."

Logic suddenly collapsed in the ruins of its towering lunacy as she saw what he meant.

She whispered, "Henry! That's absurd."

"It might not be me that slips," he said. "It might be Albrecht. Well, are we all ready to carry on?"

The ledge continued alongside the river for some distance, and they made good progress, impeded only by occasional places where it narrowed sharply, and one stretch where it was piled up with loose rubble. Albrecht continually clicked his torch on and off, and their eyes learned the trick of photographing the flashes, to be acted on by their hands and feet. After ten minutes or a quarter of an hour they passed a narrow side gallery on their right; Albrecht stopped while they came abreast of him, but Henry was insistent on following the upstream course of the river.

They had traveled perhaps as far again when the ledge ended in a tangle of broken rock dropping down to the bubbling water. Albrecht tried to climb over it, but his attempt only set off a slide of stones into the river.

He said, "We could go back and try that gallery which we passed?"

"Not if I can help it," Henry said grimly. "Keep that light on me for a minute, Albrecht."

He sat on the ledge so that his feet dangled in the water, and gradually eased himself down. The water level crept upward, but when at last he let go of the rock and stood up, bracing himself against the current, the water was still some distance below the top of his rubber boots.

"Right," he called. "You next, Sinner."

Cynthia and then Albrecht joined him in the river, and they continued their trek upstream. But it was ten times harder now, with the sullen weight of water impeding them. The new strain told heavily on their bodies, already suffering under the effects of fatigue and lack of nourishment. In addition, the chill of the water gradually seeped through the rubber boots to their feet and legs.

At last, Cynthia halted, resting her left side against the inward arch of the rock. Conscious of the added pull on the rope, Albrecht turned around and flashed the torch on her. She did not look up. She was aware of Henry's coming and standing beside her, but all these things were unimportant in comparison with the tiredness and cold and hunger that shrieked in her mind.

Henry said, "What's up, Sinner?"

She still made no reply.

"It shouldn't be long before we find somewhere we can rest."

132

Albrecht had come back. He said, "She is too weary? Is it possible that we can help her, one on each side?"

Henry said, "Sinner! You've got to make an effort to get going. Come on, now."

"We could help her," Albrecht repeated.

Henry stared at him. "Don't leave that light on when we're not on the move." Darkness fell round them again. His voice was harsh. "She's dead tired, I know, but so are we. If we put that kind of strain on ourselves before it's absolutely necessary, it's probable that you and I will go under first—and then she's finished anyway."

Their voices came to her through the cotton wool of her exhaustion. Henry's appeals and Albrecht's suggestions for helping her were both ineffectual, but the objectivity of Henry's final rejoinder made an impression. The fact that he spoke of her in this way—as though she were a stranger, or an animal even—burned through the cotton wool and set resentment flickering. It was enough to let her break out of the paralysis of indifference and fatigue.

She straightened up. "All right. I can go on for a bit longer."

"That's good," Henry said. "Lead on, Albrecht."

As she plodded and stumbled forward, the desire to surrender, to stop struggling and let the river take her where it willed, began to rise again, like the anticipation of a secret pleasure. But they would not let her; they were both determined to keep her, along with themselves, in this purgatorial treadwheel of featureless water and rock and blackness.

If only she were not roped . . . She told herself how easy it would be, between the flashes of light, to let herself slip silently away. It would be too late to do anything by the time they knew of it. She wondered at her earlier terror of death by drowning. Any kind of death was peace.

She remembered the knife Henry had given her with a leap of joy as positive as the resentment which had spurred her into moving again. She could cut herself free. . . . She had begun to fumble for it in her pocket before she realized it would not help her. As soon as she cut one rope, one of them would know of it. They were jailers, one before and one behind, and they would not let her go free.

For a moment she hated them both as, she thought, she had never hated anyone before. She wanted to cry out against the injustice of their tyranny, but she no longer had the strength to cry—to do anything but lurch, one

133

foot pushed forward after the other. She was in a child-hood nightmare again, where somehow the rooted feet had to be made to move.

She heard Albrecht call something, and heard Henry reply, but the cotton wool was back again, stifling all noise but the relentless hammering roar of the river. She contin-ued to stumble forward, and found herself being held by someone. It must be Albrecht, she decided, as he had a torch in one hand. Someone else came up and also helped to support her. Henry, she thought, proud of being able to work that out—Henry, my husband.

She was aware of their lifting her, and suddenly vividly conscious that there was no more pressure against her legs. They let her down, and there was bliss in feeling flat rock beneath her, supporting her body. All her dull anger against the two men went, replaced by a wondering grati-tude that they should have helped her to this contentment.

Henry said, "We're still having some luck. I don't think Cynthia could have gone another ten yards. For that mat-ter, I don't think I could."

"We are all so tired," Albrecht said. "I think we must sleep here."

"I'm not sure about that. I was thinking in terms of half an hour's rest."

"We must have proper rest, if we are to face the river once more."

"Shine your torch around."

Cynthia opened her eyes to see the yellowing light reflected from a ceiling only a few feet above her. They were in a kind of alcove that lay alongside the river. It measured about twelve feet square, and the ceiling ran down at an angle to meet the floor.

Albrecht said, "The torch is nearly done."

"If the river rises suddenly," Henry said, "we'll be drowned like rats."

The light clicked off. "If we try to go on without first sleeping, I think we will drown anyway. But it does not matter. If we rest for half an hour, then we shall sleep. I think Cynthia sleeps already."

Whatever they decided, they would not make her move from here. No bed had ever been as welcoming as this bare rock. Sleep was so near that it was a luxury to hold it off for a moment. Only a moment.

"All right," Henry said. "We stay. We'd better huddle up as close as possible—being on top of the river will keep us cooler than we were last night."

The two men settled themselves on either side of her. Their bodies, beside hers, were warm and reassuring. Everything was all right, after all; even the sharp pain of hunger was dulled by her tiredness.

Drifting in the monstrous suburbs of sleep, she was vaguely glad that she lay between the two men, rather than having Heather next to her. Heather, she had found, tended to kick. But she hoped, with her last conscious thought, that Heather and Peter were warm and safe as she was—and wondering why she should hope that, she fell asleep.

One of the first thoughts when she awoke was also of Heather and Peter, but one of clear remembrance, a thought of pity and horror. A few feet away the river still raged against its confining channel of rock. She realized that soon they would have to continue their struggle against it, and knew that although her mind had been cleared and refreshed by sleep, her body—barely nourished in more than thirty-six hours of physical strain and discomfort— was weak even now, before they started.

She called softly, "Henry?"

There was no reply for a moment. Then Albrecht said, "I think he still sleeps."

"Oh. Could I have the torch? I want to go down to the river."

When she came back, she let the light fall on Henry's face; it was no more than a dim yellow glow now and unlikely to disturb him. She could see that he was asleep. Albrecht was sitting up against the rock a few feet away. She went over and sat beside him.

"Your torch."

He took it from her. "It can be thrown away. It gives less light than a candle would."

"What time is it?"

"It is nearly three o'clock. We have slept long."

"In the morning?"

"Yes. In the morning."

"Almost time for a new day to begin, outside."

They were speaking very quietly so as not to disturb Henry, and she did not immediately catch what he said next.

"What was that?" she asked.

"Our last day down here."

"I'd like to think so."

"It must be. We have good light for four or five hours, and then two candles, some matches, and a lighter. But

135

even if it were not for that, it is also true that we are all the time growing weaker. We will have less strength today than yesterday—tomorrow, none, I think."

After a brief silence she said, "You wanted death, didn't you, Albrecht? It was—those other two who had everything to live for."

"It is strange. I wanted death; or rather, I had ceased to want to live. I thought there was nothing which could bring that desire back to me. Yet now, when death is so close, I want to live."

"Perhaps it's just that even death you must have on your own terms—you can't bear to have it imposed on you."

"No. There is more. I want to live." His hand found her sleeve and traveled down to her wrist. "I love you, Cynthia. I want you to marry me."

Although he had spoken softly, she said, "Hush!"

He said, still quietly, "Why? We do not need to hide things any more. If we die, we die together, and if we live, we can live together also."

"You take it for granted I would marry you."

"Not for my own merits, but for yours. I have told you before: you are not a light woman."

"All right, I love you; we both know that. But there is something you must not forget."

"This is—?"

"That Henry and I have been married for sixteen years. We could almost have been grandparents. If we are all going to die down here, he must not be hurt. It would be wicked and senseless."

"We are not going to die," Albrecht said. "We are going to live. And we shall have children, you and I, and grandchildren."

She made no reply. They sat together silently, their hands joined, for what seemed a long time, before they heard Henry move and then saw the beam of his headlamp snap on. The beam traveled around to cover them.

"Oh, you're there," Henry said.

Cynthia said, "Trying to ease our aches by sitting up."

"Have you been awake long?"

"Not long."

Henry looked at his watch. "I seem to have overslept. We'll have to skip breakfast."

She tried to smile at the little joke, but could not manage it.

Henry said, "Cheer up, Sinner. It'll soon be all over."

136

"Will it?"

"Yes. We'll make it today. How's your torch, Albrecht?"

Albrecht switched it on; the filament could be seen, glowing red.

"Not much good, is it?" Henry asked. "I'd better go first on the line today, then."

"This can be thrown away?"

"Unless you want it as a souvenir."

Henry began roping himself on the lifeline, and passed it on to Cynthia and Albrecht. Albrecht tossed the torch into the river; the water swallowed it up. When they were ready, Henry said,

"And so we say goodbye to our little nest, somewhere inside the Frohnberg."

"Darling," Cynthia said, "please—I'm not feeling at all facetious."

"Actually," Henry said, "it's Albrecht who ought to be cracking jokes, isn't it? The situation is desperate, but not serious—isn't that right?"

Albrecht said, "I am one of the solemn Austrians. There are those, too."

"Well," Henry said, "are we ready for the river?"

Cynthia felt herself shivering at the prospect. She managed to nod her head and saw Henry ease himself down from the alcove until he was standing in the water. He walked out several feet and then turned, so that the light illumined the point of entry for the other two.

Cynthia got down and felt again the cold moving heaviness pulling in her legs. Albrecht followed after her. Then Henry turned round, and they set off upstream.

Henry tried to economize on the torch battery, as Albrecht had done the previous day, by continually switching it on and off; but, since it was set in the helmet, it was more difficult for him to do this. As a result, the illumination was less satisfactory. There were longer periods of blackness, and in one of them Cynthia stumbled and almost fell.

She called, in protest, "Can't you give us a little better light, Henry?"

"I could, but I don't think it's advisable on the margin we have. Stick it out. I think there's a place where we can get out of the water just ahead."

The place, when they reached it, proved a disappointment. There was a fairly broad ledge alongside the river but, like the alcove in which they had spent the night, it

137

was only a matter of a few feet long. There was nothing to do but continue along the river bed; and now their task was made more difficult by the fact that they were in a stretch where the river tumbled down an incline. They were forced to climb uphill in addition to forcing their way against the strong current.

It could not be more than an hour since they had set off, and already Cynthia could feel herself weakening. Light for four or five hours, and then two candles and a few matches . . . But she wondered if she had the strength for even another hour's traveling in these conditions. She lurched forward as her foot went into a pothole, and had to pull herself back; as she did so, the current almost dragged her off her feet.

They had become used to the constant background of noise from the river, but as they struggled forward, Cynthia was aware of a new deeper note in it. It was a note which became increasingly more compelling. When Henry halted and waited for the others to come up with him, she had guessed what it was before he spoke.

"A fall," he said, "and not very far ahead. By the sound of it, something pretty considerable. It's going to be difficult to hear each other. We'd better tug on the rope if we want to attract attention."

Cynthia said wearily, "And when we reach it, what then? Just climb up?"

"We'll have to see."

The sound gradually grew louder but then, as though they had turned an invisible corner, it quite suddenly became a savage din, isolating each of them in a cocoon of deafness. The noise had changed its character also; its reverberation echoed in vaster spaces, as though the solid mountain rock about them had opened up into a hollow resonant bowl.

Henry flashed his light up, and Cynthia saw that something like that had actually happened. They had come out of the tunnel into the bottom of a broad shaft, stretching to some unguessable zenith. Right ahead of them was the waterfall. It plunged in a narrow cascade to a small foaming pool, and from there escaped toward the tunnel.

They huddled together and tried to talk—it was necessary to shout to be intelligible.

Henry said, "We'll have to climb out of it."

"But how?"

"We might as well get out of the river, anyway."

138

Albrecht failed to hear him. Henry cupped his hands, and bawled, "We'll get out of the river first."

It was something, at least, to be on dry land, to be free of the constant cold drag of the water against their legs.

"You can rest here," Henry told her. "Albrecht and I will scout around."

When they had freed her from the line, she lay back and tried to rest. The floor was covered at this point with thousands of small round pebbles; she ran her fingers among them as though she were a child at the seashore. Occasionally a flash from Henry's torch would illuminate a vista up the great shaft above. Its walls were terrifyingly sheer, as though they had been machined out of the rock. And all the time the clangor of the crashing water echoed and re-echoed against them. It was impossible to rest. She tried covering her ears with the palms of her hands, but the only effect was to make the noise beat more inwardly. In the end, she got to her feet, and made her way through the blackness toward the occasional light of the torch.

When she came on the two men, Henry said something to her which was clearly a rebuke, although she could only pick out a word here and there. Probably, she thought, he was objecting to her having wandered away from the place where they had left her, risking the possiblility of being lost or falling down some still deeper shaft.

She made no attempt to reply; it would have been difficult enough in normal conditions to explain how she felt. Instead, she said to Albrecht, bending close to him, "Have you found anything?"

He pointed up the wall by which they stood. They were nearly paralledl with the fall, and close enough for her to feel the damp feathers of spray against her face. But the wall, when Henry's light shone on it, looked utterly unpromising. It was almost as sheer as anywhere else; the surface was dimpled and rugose but the line of pitch was no less severe.

Henry began hammering an iron into the surface. She could see the hammer striking against the end of the iron, but the sound was barely audible in the din caused by the hammer of water striking its anvil of rock. An iron was driven in, and another. Henry began to mount on his iron ladder, hammering fresh steps in as he went.

She shouted to Albrecht, "It's hopeless! He hasn't enough irons."

All she could make out from his reply was something about "ledge." She did not pay very much attention. It oc-

139

curred to her that, if they had to die down in this warren of tunnels and caves, of rivers and lakes and waterfalls, this was the worst place of all in which to make an end. Even their little alcove beside the river would have been preferable to here, where surely the noise would drive them mad before exhaustion finally claimed them. And yet, she could not face the idea of going back down the river again; back toward those tortured depths where the bodies of Heather and Peter had now, perhaps, eddied to rest.

The noise went on and on. Albrecht took her arm, but she disregarded him. She thought of screaming, but her scream would be meaningless and ineffectual. Then light beamed down on them from above. She looked up and saw that Henry was coming back down the irons.

He did not come all the way down. Standing on the third iron, he made a gesture to Albrecht of pulling an iron out of the wall, and pointed to the two beneath him. Albrecht succeeded in wrenching them free and then, at another sign from Henry, tossed them in turn up to him. The second one he missed, but caught it when it was thrown again. They saw him climb back up the rock face, the light going ahead of him, leaving them in the darkness, exposed to the constantly crashing cymbals of an infernal smithy.

Albrecht shook her wrist and said something, pointing upward. She looked, and there was only darkness. That could only mean that Henry had reached a ledge or a shaft up there somewhere . . . soon, in that case, the ladder would come snaking down and they could climb—a part of the way at least—out of this pit of thunder.

She waited for the ladder, straining her eyes up into the night which would never, throughout the earth's ages, break into dawn—for the ladder or for the flash of light which would herald the ladder. Nothing happened. She tried counting seconds and minutes, but the steady pulsing fury of the fall confused and distracted her.

She shouted to Albrecht, "Do you think something's happened to him?"

It was difficult to tell whether he had understood her. He squeezed her arm reassuringly, and said something which she, for her part, completely failed to hear.

Could he have left them, abandoned them, she wondered? Perhaps, just up there, he had found a tunnel leading out onto a green Austrian hillside and walked away into the sunshine, into the world of light and peace, leaving them to their adulterous' hell. When she put it like that, she wanted to laugh at her own absurdity, but if she once started laughing she was not sure that she would be able to stop. She hung on a precipice of mind, overlooking chasms of hysteria as deep and sunless as the one in which they now were.

She was so engrossed in contemplation of this that when the signal came she was unprepared for it. Albrecht gripped her arm again and she saw him pointing upward. A beam of light arrowed across the shaft; it seemed a long way above them. A few moments later, the ray was directed vertically downward, and in its narrow brilliance they could see the electron ladder. It did not quite reach the ground.

By signs, Albrecht indicated that Cynthia should take one of the coils of rope as well as the other ladder. The second coil of rope dropped down parallel with the ladder, and he saw that it was made fast around her. He himself had the remaining irons, the acetylene lamp, and the folded boat to carry with him. In addition, he would have to wrench the irons out of the wall during his climb.

As she climbed there was, at least, the relief of escaping from the center of the hurricane of noise toward its periphery. But the climb itself was far from easy. The face was more wrinkled and pitted than it had seemed from below. At one moment she would find herself swinging free in space, and at the next straining for a toehold where the bars of electron rested hard against the smooth rock.

She had expected that, as with their first climb, out of the low-roofed cave into the cave of stalactites, it would be a matter of coming out at the top onto a level surface —another cave, perhaps, or, at any rate, a ledge which would be flat and of some width. The truth was very different.

It was as though she had climbed the vertical wall of a house, to be faced with the sharp angle of the roof. For as far ahead as she could see in glimpses afforded by Henry's headlamp, the slope stretched upward and away. Over on the left, plainly, the river rolled tumultuously down that same slope toward its fall. Henry dragged her up beside him on the slope.

"I've chiseled out a couple of footholds for you," he told her. "Lie forward against the rock, and get your toes into them."

She shuddered. "That drop . . ."

141

"Forget about it. Try not to think of anything at all until we're ready to move on."

She looked up. "We've got to scale that?"

"It's not as bad as it looks. Once we get away from the edge, it won't bother you."

She did as he had told her. Twisting her head to look around, she was able to see Henry making his arrangements to receive Albrecht. He had made footholds for himself almost on the edge, and provided himself with 'an iron as a handhold. From this he stretched out perilously, so as to look down the face and at the same time light the way up for Albrecht. She found that, for fear, she could not watch him. She let her face rest against the cool hard rock.

With each surmounting of an obstacle, the mind swung, naturally enough, toward optimism and contemplation of the possibility of finding a way out. Even now, with the obstacle only half conquered and a possibly terrifying climb directly ahead, there was this reaction—it was such a relief to be away from the point of impact of the waterfall.

Here their needs were physical and urgent, summed up in one aim: to escape death. What would happen if the threat of death receded, and the threats and promises of life, with its confusions and half certainties, were once again paramount? She would leave Henry and go to Albrecht. She wondered how it would affect him. He would not, she thought, marry again. Probably he would go back to the youth clubs in which, before their marriage, he had found his greatest interest. She thought of him growing into middle age, surrounded by young people, teaching boys how to tie the right knots in ropes, listening to young men and smiling. She would need to be certain of her love for Albrecht to abandon him to that.

Her marriage had been something she had taken for granted, as one of the unquestioned things in life. Now that it had broken up, under a stress previously unimaginable, she had no illusions that her relationship with Albrecht could take its place. She would marry Albrecht, but not as a free agent. It was something in which she could expect to find joy, but never contentment. The English wife, abandoning her dull English husband for a foreign count —when we think ourselves most secure in our maturity, life can turn us back into spiritual schoolgirls.

Henry helped Albrecht up beside them. Cynthia and Albrecht were already on the rope, and Henry now tied himself on in the lead positon.

142

He said, "Try to follow me as exactly as you can—I may have to hammer out footholds in places. Don't look back, and don't think of anything except the stretch immediately ahead. Give me a call when you want a rest or some light—I'll try to flash down to you as much as possible."

Cynthia followed him up the slope. It was disconcerting at first, and a couple of times they had to halt while Henry chiseled holes in the rock, but after that it got easier; partly as she became accustomed to the process of dragging herself up the slope and partly because the slope itself began to flatten out slightly. The real enemy was fatigue; it swayed in on her like a fog if she thought of the depths beneath them and the possible heights which they had yet to climb. It was some consolation, though not much, to think of Henry who, having already been burdened with so much greater effort than she and Albrecht, was still taking by far the greater strain.

There was another steeper pitch to traverse, but after that the slope eased again, and went on easing. At last Henry stood up and waved his hand for them to do the same. They continued climbing, but with no more difficulty than in climbing the side of an ordinary hill.

Almost simultaneously, there was a roof above them and a stretch in front which, although pitted and broken, was, in the main, level. Here, too, began outcrops of stalactites and brilliant crystal clusters, but they paid no attention to them, their sense of wonder effectively blanketed by weariness and hunger.

They found themselves in a cave of considerable width and length, but with a relatively low roof. In places, stalactite spears, hanging down toward stalagmitic growths, had joined with them to form columns. Here and there the roof dripped water, showing that the stalactites were still active.

They came on a colony of gypsum bushes, white and spiky and delicately fragile in the light from Henry's headlamp, and plunged through them heedlessly, their heavy boots breaking and scattering the efflorescences of crystal. The pace Henry was setting was a very fast one. In the end, Cynthia protested, "You'll have to let me take a breather. I can't keep it up."

Henry stopped. "All right." He switched off the light in his helmet. "As long as we don't waste light, it doesn't matter too much."

They sat together by a pillar of rock, surfaced with sta-

143

lactite. The ground underfoot, Cynthia noticed, was relatively soft, even mushy. She commented on this to Henry.

"Probably mud again," he told her. "Very likely another intermittent water passage."

"Is that good?"

"Mud? Yes. It shows there's a channel to the surface. But it may be a long way away. Rivers can carry mud for miles."

"Yes, of course. We found mud down by the lake, didn't we? But at least we're still going in the right direction."

"Yes."

There was silence for a time. Cynthia said idly, "Rather a strange smell. Do you notice it?"

"Your nose is keener than mine. It's probably the mud."

"A musky smell."

"Musk!" Henry said. He flicked his headlamp on, and she saw that the mud was grayish in color, speckled with darker fragments. Abruptly the light was directed up toward the ceiling overhead. It was brown and seemed somehow to shiver in the light. A part of it moved, and she ducked her head away.

Henry said, "Do you have any idea what we're sitting on?"

His voice was happier than it had been for a long time. He did not wait for her to reply.

"Bat guano," he said.

"How horrible."

The light shone full on her face. Henry pulled her to him and kissed her. "How wonderful."

"You mean . . ."

"This is a bat cave—the place where they rest during the day. We must be near the surface. Do you think you're ready to go on?"

She said, marveling, "Are we so near?"

"It's the first time we've had a real reason for hope."

They advanced along the cave, with Henry throwing the beam of light from side to side in survey. After a time, the cave narrowed, and then, fairly sharply, turned to the left. Henry switched his lamp off again. He said, "Look all around you."

Their eyes searched the darkness. It was Albrecht who said, "Over there."

Although they could not see the direction in which he was pointing, the sound of his voice gave them some idea.

144

Cynthia saw it—a lighter patch against the unrelieved black.

Henry said doubtfully, "Not what I'd hoped for, but we might as well have a look at it."

The patch gradually brightened as they approached, but even when they were almost on top of it, it remained dim. It was a hole, a couple of feet in diameter, almost level with the floor. Henry knelt, and poked his head in. Then he withdrew, turned about, and eased himself through backwards.

"What is it?" Cynthia asked.

"I'm not sure. But it's only a few feet drop—I can see enough for that. Follow me through."

11.

CYNTHIA dropped backward through the hole, and Henry caught her and steadied her. She looked around as Albrecht passed the ropes and ladders through, and then came through himself.

They were in a place of deep gloom, but it appeared light after the blackness from which they had come. There was a rank smell here, more pungent and nauseating than that of the bat guano. The hole was an opening in a vast overhang stretching above them. Her eyes followed its shadowy outline for what seemed an immense distance. Right at the top there was another round glow, much smaller than the one they had followed inside the cave, but also much brighter. She stared at it for several moments before she was able to believe what was obviously the case: the glow came from the world outside. It was the glow of sunlight.

She clutched Henry's arm. "Look!"

He nodded. "I've seen it."

"Then we're almost free!"

He helped Albrecht down. "Almost."

Henry switched on his light and directed it round about. It was obvious that once again they were at the foot of a vast gulf, but this time a gulf with an opening to the surface. On this side, the wall ran up in an overhang that appeared to funnel its way right up to the distant circle of

145

day. On the other, it came down in a more or less straight drop. And at the foot . . .

Cynthia turned her head away, sickened. She knew now what the new smell was. Facing them on the other side of the bottom of the hole was a grotesque pile of carcasses in various stages of decay, with bones showing through the rotting flesh.

Henry said to Albrecht, "There can't be all that many places like this. Have you any idea where we are?"

Albrecht said slowly, "I think that I know. I think we have come through the hill to the other side. There is such a place as this, and I have not heard of another."

Cynthia asked, "What kind of a place is it?"

"The country people call it a bottomless pit; for them anything that is too deep to see the bottom is called bottomless. They use it to be rid of dead animals, and sometimes living animals that are diseased. Bats swarm out from it at dusk, and in again at dawn. At one time, the country people believed that they were inhabited by the souls of the damned, but I do not think that is believed today."

Henry made a gesture toward the heap of putrescence that faced them.

"Where is this place?"

"About two kilometers from Liedl."

"Then the caves are connected!"

Cynthia asked, "What about getting out?"

There was a pause before Henry said, "The only way to get out is to go farther in."

"Farther in?"

He flashed the light up and around the walls. "We couldn't possibly scale those. But over there"—the torch beam gave a sickening glimpse of the hill of carrion— "those carcasses are in front of a cave mouth. If you look at the top, you can see the top of the cave."

Cynthia said, "Are you suggesting not only that having caught a glimpse of daylight we're to go back underground again, but also that we're to wade through that filth?"

"I think we'll have to."

"It's absurd. Tell him we can't do it, Albrecht."

"Sinner," Henry said gently, "what else do you suggest?"

"We can stay here—take it in turns to call out for help. There's a good chance of someone hearing us."

Henry said, "If someone had his head stuck over the

146

hole, listening very carefully, he might hear all three of us shouting together. But that's not likely to happen."

"Albrecht said that the country people come here to—to throw down dead animals."

"Not every day—and I don't suppose they stay once the carcass has been thrown down. Even if one did, and heard something, he would think it was an animal—or a devil."

She said desperately, "I don't care. Albrecht, tell him we must stay."

"At any rate, we might as well have your opinion, Albrecht," said Henry.

Albrecht said, "I do not know. Henry is right. They would not be likely to hear us and, if they did, it is almost certain they would pay no attention. But it would be terrible to go back in there again, when we have been within sight of the open."

"We have no choice," Henry insisted. "If we're within a couple of kilometers of Liedl, we're probably almost on top of the Liedl caves. It's no good being blinded by that little patch of daylight overhead. We're as far from being rescued down here as we were when we were crossing the lake. It isn't very nice to go into the caves again, especially with only a few hours' light left, but we've got to do it."

"You go," Cynthia said, "if you feel you have to. Leave Albrecht and me here."

"If you like, we can leave you. Then, providing we get through, we can arrange to have you picked up from here. But I may need Albrecht's help."

Her "No" was involuntary. She added weakly, "I don't want to be left on my own."

Henry said, "Your life's your own when we get out, Sinner. You know that. But as things are, you're still my wife."

She asked him helplessly, "You know?"

"I've known for some days. Heather said something—about Albrecht. It doesn't matter what it was. I don't think you've had enough practice at hiding things; as soon as I began to watch you, it was fairly clear."

Albrecht said, "It is better that you should know."

"Is it? I suppose so. Anyway, it doesn't matter. Nothing matters just now, except getting out of here. You're going to do as I tell you, aren't you?"

Cynthia said nothing.

Albrecht said, "I think that is the wisest thing. Without you, we should have been lost ten times over. I do not

147

want to go back down there, but it is you who must decide."

"In that case," Henry said, "there's no point in wasting time." He turned to Cynthia. "I suppose if Albrecht goes, you want to go? You don't want to stay here?"

She made a sign of negation. She was still under the shock of realizing that Henry knew—had known throughout their ordeal—of what lay between Albrecht and herself. She roped herself automatically and picked up the coiled ladder and the rope.

The shock helped her somewhat over the next, nauseating obstacle. A part of her was insulated by it from the sick horror which automatically arose as they approached the festering heap of putrescence behind which the arc of a cave mouth could be seen. Henry, after inspecting it, led them away to the right, where the bones and rotting flesh did not rise so high. The beam of his headlamp picked out the individual parts of the pile with horrifying clarity—the rotting eyeless skull of a cow stared up, with one horn capped by an old tin: presumable some boy had thrown the tin down to test the depths, and chance had made it land on the upstretched horn. The grim coincidence of this was ironical as well as hideous.

But she still saw it with an eye of almost casual detachment. She was thinking of Henry—trying to see him as he was. She had thought of him conventionally; as, before falling in love with Albrecht, she had thought of herself. In the terms of that convention, it had been easy to see him as the betrayed husband, happily ignorant of having been betrayed. Now she must reckon with the fact that he had known about it all the time; and that he had kept the knowledge to himself, giving her no hint of it, during his long drawn-out struggle to lead them through the caves to safety.

She had already been surprised in herself. She had to admit to an even greater surprise in Henry.

This shock and preoccupation allowed her to see the things they were approaching without too great a nausea; but it was different when, following Henry, she felt the obscene mixture squelch under her boots. Then, abruptly, she wanted to be sick. She stood for a moment, with the bile rising in her throat, trying to prevent herself from retching.

By stopping she impeded Henry's progress as well. He called back sharply, "Sinner! You mustn't stop. Keep moving and try not to think about it. We'll be over it soon."

148

She forced herself to go on, closing her mind as well as she could to the smell and the sight of things glimpsed in the slowly traveling brightness of the torch. But there was no way of blotting out the sensation of her feet treading it all down, of the slither and crunch beneath her. Once she slipped, and for a long unbearable moment thought that she was going to fall. The panic that this induced was succeeded, as she regained her footing, by such relief that she advanced the next few yards without being aware of it.

After that, she was over the top and going down the other side. Light dazzled in her face, and she caught sight of Henry's arm stretched out toward her. He pulled her to him, and she stood on solid rock.

While Henry helped Albrecht through, she began to retch in earnest. There was nothing in her stomach, so that she could not vomit. The spasms passed off after a time and she rested her face against the wall of the cave in her exhaustion.

She was aware of Henry standing by her. Albrecht put his arm around her shoulder. He said, "We should not stay here, Cynthia. It is best to get away from this place as soon as we can."

She nodded wearily. "I'm all right now. I can go on."

For tens of centuries the shaft they had just left must have collected bodies; either in deliberate disposal by men or through the ordinary accident of animals' falling to their death. The carcasses rotted in the cave mouth, and the fluids of their putrefaction ran down the gentle slope inside toward the nearest watercourse. In addition the accumulation of more recent bodies, by a slow build-up of pressure, pushed down the bones already leached by dissolution.

They walked down the dark gallery of a natural history museum, its specimens intertwined in the disorder of the centuries. The torch beam lit on fragments of bone, seemingly whole skeletons, jutting antlers. Henry rested the light briefly on one great skull.

"Cave bear," he said. "He probably came from inside, not down the shaft. It's a good sign. It probably means the caves are extensive on this side."

The trail of bones ended, and there was just the gentle slope, leading down. The cave had widened into a broad and lofty hall. The going was good, and Henry kept the pace fast. Cynthia was conscious of the strain but made no protest. As they went on, the minutes were ticking away

149

which would at last leave them in darkness—lost beyond hope of safety.

The hall ended in a minor confluence of galleries. There were at least three in which it was possible to walk without stooping. Henry decided on the right-hand one; not only did it show an immediate upward slope, but there was also the sound of water higher up. It was, Cynthia noted with relief, not the wild cataracting thunder that they had encountered previously, but an almost gentle sound, reminiscent of a stream beside an English lane.

They found the stream where the gallery ran into another at right angles. It was as placid as its sound had promised, flowing calmly between ribbed and runneled walls that bore witness to an earlier forgotten violence. They rested briefly by its edge, the light switched off, and then set out again upstream.

Ten minutes later, they had traced the stream to its impenetrable source. It welled out of solid jaws of rock, not more than six inches wide. They stared at it, until Henry switched the light off.

"Then we must go back," Albrecht said.

They started back in silence. Cynthia watched the flashes of light from the torch. She had the idea they were less bright than they had been. She was thinking of this when Henry stopped, directing the light on a hole in the gallery wall. She wondered if he had noticed it too.

"I'm going to try this," Henry said.

"Try? You mean, to get through the hole? Surely it's much too small."

Henry's voice was strained. "It won't do any harm to see. I don't want us to go any farther back than is absolutely necessary."

With Albrecht, she watched him wriggle into the hole, his body, as he progressed, cutting off more and more of the light, until they were left in darkness. They stood close together, aware of each other's breathing and of the cheerful chuckling noise of the stream.

"Darling," she asked him, "what do you think?"

"I think that we shall get through. I am sure of it."

"We're running it close."

The lifeline jerked tight. She heard Henry's voice, muffled and indistinguishable, and called up the hole to him.

"What was that?"

Although still muffled, she could understand what he said next: "I think it will go. I want you to come in after me. Push the stuff in front of you."

150

She said to Albrecht, "If we all get stuck in that rat trap . . ."

"It will not happen. Come. I will help you to get in."

She felt the solid rock close around her, touching her all along her body, with intimacy and ghastly strength. She inched her way forward, responding to Henry's tugs on the line. She went, as he had told her before, on her side, but several yards in the pipe closed down, and she had to crawl forward painfully, her face against the rock and the rock pressing also against the top of her head.

For the greater part she was in utter blackness. The absence of light, unpleasant under normal circumstances, was terrifying when added to the close-pressing confinement of the rock about her. Her mind, strained out of reason, offered no bar to the most absurd of fantasies—she was crawling into Hell, and Hell itself was no more than an endless black tube, narrowing, narrowing, but never quite squeezing out the existence of the damned. As she went deeper, she dragged Albrecht after her into damnation. A thin line would link them for all eternity, but that was all the link they would have. They would never be together. . . .

The fantasy engaged and obsessed her. It was only when a pull from in front made her think of Henry that she was able to escape from it. It was impossible to imagine Henry as leading them into Hell. Whatever she and Albrecht might have deserved had nothing to do with him.

But breaking out of her metaphysical nightmare only made her more immediately conscious of the physical one. She felt slivers of rock scraping against her face. She threshed desperately to get away from them, and got an arm wedged in front of her. Realizing she was stuck, she struggled the harder, and her struggling pinned her down more firmly.

Henry's muffled voice came back: "What's the matter?"

She cried, "I can't move!"

He said urgently, "Stop fighting it. Don't do anything at all except count up to ten. Slowly. Then move back a bit. Make it slow and easy. Now—count."

She obeyed his instructions and found that it was quite easy to free herself. But the prospect of going on, wriggling like a snake through stony burrows, unnerved her.

She called up to Henry, "I don't think I can carry on with it."

"Stick it."

"I can't. The whole thing's so pointless. Henry—I don't want to die in here."

"It's getting wider just ahead. Only a few more yards. Come on now, Sinner."

She believed him, and by the time she understood that he had been deceiving her, that particular crisis was past. She found it possible to go on squirming forward in his wake. Where he had gone, she could follow. And then, after ages, it was wider, the rock was no longer pressing against her on all sides. In the end, she could crawl on hands and knees. It made her feel human again.

The pipe turned into a gallery. It was neither wide nor high, but it led upward. It was also damp, with drops of water oozing through the ceiling onto them. Henry called another halt for a rest, and they crouched together. Cynthia remembered a time, when she was a girl, of crouching with boy cousins inside a small and rain-dripping tent. We were all miserable, she remembered with surprise, because it was raining.

Albrecht said, "Your headlamp, Henry—the battery is almost gone?"

"I give it another five minutes."

"And then?" Cynthia asked.

"The acetylene lamp."

"And then?" she whispered.

"The candles."

She said, "I would rather go on. We'll have plenty of time to rest afterwards, won't we?"

When the headlamp had faded to a dim glow that showed nothing ahead, Henry lit the acetylene lamp. Cynthia remembered what he had said: about an hour's charge. Unlike the torches, that really meant an hour—the lamp could not be flicked on and off for economizing. They had been wandering for two days and nights in this warren of caves; it was futile to imagine that another hour would see them to safety.

After that, there would be the blundering about for an hour or so with the candles and then, presumably, the matches struck one by one and, in between, a blind groping forward. At the end, there would only be the blind groping.

They came to an intersection with another gallery, somewhat wider, and Henry took the left-hand fork. For a time they traveled under fairly easy conditions, making as much speed as possible. Cynthia felt herself panting from the exertion, and had the beginning of a stitch in her side.

152

Another wet patch slowed them up. The ceiling began to drip in earnest, and soon there was a small rivulet running down the middle of the gallery. It was by observing the direction in which it flowed that Cynthia realized they were now traveling down hill.

She had little time to brood over this. The roof of the gallery leaked at an ever-increasing rate, and the rivulet underfoot swelled to a stream. After five or ten minutes they were all soaking wet. Her wet hair dropped forward over her eyes, and she had to brush it back. Her boots splashed through the deepening stream, which soon covered the entire width of the gallery.

The acetylene lamp lit up the drops of water, falling like rain, the streaming walls, and the heavy flow of water underfoot. In places the roof dipped low; another nine inches and they would be forced to crawl on hands and feet through the stream. If that happened, the heavy rubber boots which had so far protected them would become waterlogged, and a hindrance.

But instead of this, another hazard presented itself. They heard it in the distance, and the too familiar sound grew louder and more unmistakable as they went on: the noise of falling water. It could only be the stream along which they were traveling; somewhere, not far ahead, it must plunge down into depths which, by the sound of it, were considerable.

Then, thought Cynthia, we have come to our end—really to our end.

When she thought the drop must be right under her feet, Henry stopped. He held up the lamp, and she saw that for the next few feet there was a sharp tumbling descent. Beyond that there was a final lip, over which the water poured.

Henry looked around, searching for something.

She asked him, "What is it?"

"A lump of rock. It doesn't matter."

He took off his helmet, with the now useless lamp. She saw him throw it out so that it cleared the lip of the fall. They heard nothing but the continuing roar of the water.

"No luck," he said. "I didn't think we should have."

Albrecht said, "There is a ledge, I think. Up there."

Above the fall, the gallery widened out into a dome. They could see the far side, but there was no sign of any extension of the gallery in that direction. The ledge that Albrecht had pointed out ran round the bottom of the

153

dome, and appeared to peter out somewhere on the opposite side.

"Not much promise," Henry said, "but I can't think of anything better."

They watched while he drove three irons into the face of the rock, making a ladder by which he could climb up on the ledge. Once there, he called for the others to follow him.

Albrecht asked,

"The irons—how can I get them back?"

"You can get the top one. I shouldn't bother about the others. We haven't time."

They sidled along the ledge. It was not very wide, and the drop beneath them, revealed by the lamp, was precipitous. Cynthia followed Henry automatically. She had no hope now, and was no more than wearily patient of the continuing efforts of the two men to put off for a little longer the inevitable. Where the ledge ended would be the point at which they, too, must face facts. The only thing to do then would be to find their way back to some place where death could be waited for with dignity.

Henry said, "Hold it there."

"What is it?"

"I'm going to try a climb."

"Up this?"

She glanced up at the dome of rock, arching dimly overhead. A fly might scale it, but only to find as painful a descent on the other side to a gulf of splashing water.

"There's a break over there." Henry held the lamp a little higher. "Can you see it?"

Looking closely, she could see what he was talking about. At a point roughly opposite the one from which they had started, the two halves of the dome failed to meet. Between them lay something which, from their present position, was indistinguishable. It might be an escape chimney, or it might be no better than a crevice.

She understood the kind of a climb Henry had in mind. The objective, whatever it might be, lay about thirty feet from them on an upward diagonal slope. In view of the inward curve of the rock face and the fact that the ledge was not continuous all around, a series of irons hammered in to cover that diagonal offered the best—probably the only—approach. But it was horribly risky, and possibly to no purpose.

She said, "Henry, let's go back. Let's just try to find somewhere we can lie down—a dry place."

154

He looked at her for a moment without speaking. It was a look that conveyed nothing—a look searching, remembering. He said at last: "You may have to, Sinner. But wait till I've tried this. Albrecht, pass along what irons you've got."

She took the irons from Albrecht and handed them on to Henry. After that there was the waiting while he made methodical preparations and then began to hammer in the pitons. He had given her the lamp to hold. The drop beneath them plummeted down to a ledge strewn with boulders and small rocks. Water from the falling stream hit and sprayed off it.

Gradually Henry made progress across the slope of the dome. When he was halfway there, he mis-hammered an iron and it dropped, clanging against the rock, to be lost in the dim spume of water below the ledge. He took more care in placing the next one. It went in and held.

He had almost reached the limit of the span of lifeline between them, when he called down, "It's a go. There's a hole through. A couple more irons, and you can come up."

At least it might be a hole through to a cave, to a place where one could rest—and wait. When the signal came, she set out up the ladder of irons.

As she climbed, she hung the lamp on the piton at the limit of her reach, and moved it forward a step each time. The first few irons were not too hard, but then it became more and more difficult as the slope of the rock went against her.

It was only her despair and indifference, she felt, that allowed her to keep going. Once when she looked down the rock face to the funneled abyss over which she hung, her head dizzied at the sight; but the reaction was not matched by any fear, and after a moment she went on.

She crouched beside Henry at last. The flaw in the dome led to a rubble slope, the base of a new and larger cave. He had perched himself over a projecting spur of rock, but he moved further up to allow her to rest there. Albrecht was climbing the irons.

Albrecht called up, "Must we leave these, also?"

Henry said, "Yes." She saw, with astonishment, that he was able to grin. "They'll do for the next lot who travel this way."

Albrecht had nearly reached them. She looked down toward him now, watching him come up the last two or three feet. She could hear Henry, above her, shifting his

155

position to make himself more comfortable. Then there was the sudden rumble of shifting rock, and she glanced quickly upward to see what was happening.

She had a brief confused glimpse of stones falling toward her, of Henry sliding, trying to regain his balance and failing, before his body cannoned against hers as he fell down toward the gap from which they had emerged. The lamp was wrenched from her hand and clattered down the slope. She herself fell across the spur of rock. Just below her, there was a muffled cry from one of the two men, or from both, as Henry collided with Albrecht. Then a great weight pulled her downward, pinning her immovably over the spur. The breath gasped from her body, and she could only breathe in again with difficulty and pain.

There was still light. She saw now that the lamp had come to rest on a part of the ledge and had not broken. Its light fanned up to her, and showed her what had happened.

Henry, in falling, had knocked Albrecht off the irons. The two men hung side by side, like marionettes, attached to either end of the lifeline, which pinned her down to the spur of rock. They hung clear of the sheer face. She saw their hands and feet scrabble for purchase, finding none. Beneath them there was the narrow broken ledge where the lamp rested, and then the gulf of the waterfall.

Albrecht called up, "Cynthia—you are all right?"

Her words gasped. "I—can't move."

Henry said, "Sinner."

His voice sounded almost normal; the fall could not have hurt him. "There's only one thing for it. Can you reach that knife I gave you?"

"I'm not sure."

It was painful to speak; each word had to be forced out. The arc of compression twisted her body downward. Second by second her feeling of helplessness increased.

"Try to get to it, Sinner," Henry said. "You must try."

She got her hand back awkwardly toward the pocket and forced it in. Her fingers touched the end of the knife and at last pulled it clear. Getting it out, she almost dropped it.

The men had been watching her from their seesaw of rope. Henry said, "Right. Now cut yourself free."

"But if I do, you will fall."

"We're going to fall anyway. The only thing you can do is save yourself. You must do that. Cut the ropes."

156

"No!"

"Sinner, you will have to do it in the end. The longer you leave it, the worse it is for us."

She said, "What point is there in freeing myself? The lamp's out of reach. I have a candle, but you and Albrecht have the means of lighting it. I shall be left here in the dark."

"The lamp will throw up enough light for you to see your way up the slope, I think. After that—you never know what may happen. At least, it's better than this."

She struggled for breath. "And I'm to murder you and Albrecht, first?"

"If you don't, do you know what's going to happen? You will black out after a time. We shall be left hanging here."

The pain tightened across her chest. There was nothing to say, and speech itself was an agony from which she shrank.

For the first time since the fall, Albrecht spoke. His voice sounded dazed, almost disbelieving.

"I am not sure, but I think perhaps two could be saved."

"How?"

"If you cut one of the ropes, there will be only half of the weight on you, Cynthia. It is possible that you might be able to lift the other—enough so that he may get a foothold, and climb."

A silence followed. There was only the noise of the plunging water.

Then Henry said, "I think he's right. It's worth trying. You've got to do it, Sinner—you've got to cut at least one of us free. For God's sake, do it quickly, if only for the sake of the other. You won't have the strength for much longer."

She knew he was right. The weight that dragged her down seemed to get heavier and heavier. The strain plucked at her eyes; her mind was beginning to fog. She had a little time left for saving herself, and perhaps one of them.

She looked down, and saw the two men staring up at her. Their expressions were the same. They showed no hope—only fear, and love.

Opening the knife, she looked away from them, concentrating on the rope. The blade sawed against the taut nylon.

She thought at first that she would not be able to save him after all. Her strength was very low, and he could only co-operate feebly. But he made it in the end, and they collapsed together against the rock spur, exhausted and silent. It was she who had to rouse him, so that they could climb the rest of the slope into the cave. The lamp, perched on the little ledge, was beginning to burn feebly, and cast only the dimmest of lights up to show them their way.

When they had crawled to the top of the slope, she got out the candle and gave it to him to light; but his hands shook, and she had to do it herself.

She led the way through the cave, pausing at times to help him. The candle did not reveal very much, but it seemed to be a large cave; the floor was strewn with boulders of all sizes. After five or ten minutes they came to another stream and followed its banks. It appeared to run along a narrow but fairly deep channel.

He had to rest soon afterwards. She put out the candle and sat beside him, holding him against herself. Then again she had to rouse him to continue. He went for less than a quarter of an hour before he had to stop again. When she spoke to him, he made no answer. Each time it was more difficult to get him back on the move.

The flickering light of the candle showed the cave wall to have crept in toward them, and there were glimpses of an opposite wall on the other side of the stream. The cave had narrowed to a gallery, with just the stream and a narrow walk beside it.

The end came so abruptly that she almost collided with the rock. She thought at first that the gallery must have made a right-angled turn that she had missed, but looking at the stream to check this, she realized what it was. The rock came down to within an inch of the water, and the stream disappeared under that arch.

He had seen it also. He sat down by the stream and said, "Stay here."

He merely watched her while she pulled off her rubber boots. She thought of stripping completely, but some quirk of modesty prevented her. If she was to die under there, she would rather her body was clothed.

She said, "I'm going to put the candle out, and then I'm going to try diving under it. If I find a way through, I'll tug the line several times. When that happens, you must do the same."

He looked at her but said nothing.

158

"I may not manage it," she added. "If I don't, then it's goodbye." She stooped down and kissed him. "Darling, darling, I do love you."

She waded into the stream, feeling its sharp chill against her legs and the painfully jagged surface under her bare feet. As she had thought, it was fairly deep—three or four feet. She looked at the place where rock and water almost met, doused the candle and put it away in her pocket and then, waiting no longer, plunged forward head first and began swimming under water.

Without realizing it, she came up toward the surface, and the back of her head knocked against the roof. She forced herself lower, putting her hand up from time to time to feel if there was clearance. But the rock here came right down to the water; there wasn't even the inch of space that there had been at the beginning.

The strain of holding her breath was telling on her. She had passed the point at which it might have been possible to turn and go back, and it would not be long before the effort of continuing to swim forward would be too much. She put her hand up again, but this time felt no rock above her—nothing but water.

Being without orientation, her natural thought was that somehow she had been swimming down to a deeper level. She began to swim upward hastily, careless of hitting her head on a submerged roof.

But her head broke water, and she could breathe again, painful shuddering breaths. Then she swam forward slowly, on the surface. After a time, her foot scraped against the bottom. She stood up in the water, which came just above her knees.

It was not easy to light the candle again. When she had succeeded, she could see that she was in a cave that had one end—where she now stood—under water. A few feet the other way there was dry rock.

She took in the slack on the lifeline. There was not more than two or three feet. Then she began to tug at it, in a series of sharp jerks. There was no answering jerk from the other end.

She could not possibly go down under that water again, find the concealed hole, and swim through it to get him. And yet, after all that had happened, she could not leave him. She might as well go down. If the action was futile and suicidal, so was any other.

Before she prepared to dive, she gave the rope a final tug. This time, she pulled in more slack. It could only mean one of two things: either he had untied himself from the line or he was coming through after all.

Quickly she put out the candle, and got both her hands to the rope, keeping up a steady pull. There seemed to be too much resistance for it to be only a loose rope, but it was not until she had pulled in over twenty feet of it that she heard the water splash near her, and the gasp of his indrawn breath.

She said, "You're all right now. Wait. I'll light the candle and show you."

She helped him out of the water. He continued to lean on her, and she had to support him as they made their way up the cave.

He said, "Rest. We must rest."

"No. Not yet."

Her feet were being slashed by the sharp stones under foot, but the pain meant nothing beside her tiredness and his weight on her shoulder. Suddenly he stopped again.

"Darling," she said, "we must go on."

He said, "A light. Can you see it?" His voice was different.

Her own gaze had been concentrated on watching the patch of candlelight immediately in front of their feet. She looked up and saw that it was not delirium. Away to the left, there was a glow of light.

It brightened as they went toward it. Another cave was adjacent to this one, and the light was there. There was a noise, too. She could not believe that it was what it seemed.

They turned a corner, and saw them: bare light bulbs suspended from a cable running back through the cave. And she had been right about the noise. There were about a dozen people in the middle of the cave, with a man in uniform pointing things out to them—stalactites and stalagmites, the wonders of the underground world.

He faltered beside her. "Liedl," he said. Then he slumped to the ground, and she could not hold him.

She called out something, and saw them turn toward her. Her own legs were suddenly too weak to support her, and, as they hurried to her, she collapsed also. But she was still conscious. She heard the uniformed man say,

"Es muss die zwei Engländer sein!"

They lifted her up, and he spoke to her directly. "You are safe now. Where are the others? The other two English—and the Graf?"

"They're dead," she said. Her voice was flat. She looked at Henry, lying exhausted beside her.

160

Lightning Source UK Ltd.
Milton Keynes UK
UKHW022033150223
417099UK00008B/88